RESIST AND REFUSE
DECRYING THE STATE OF THE UNION

SUMMER/FALL 2017 | ISSUE #1

CONTRIBUTORS

Rebecca J. Allred
Sally Jane Black
Erin Cashier
Selena Chambers
Rachael Cowan
Sam Cowan
Thom Davidsohn
S. L. Edwards
Kurt Fawver
Cody Goodfellow
Christian Goodrich
Glenda Goyne
Nick Gucker
Jeremy Hoevenaar
Alex S Johnson
Dominique Lamssies
Jake Marley
Anya Martin
Joseph F. Nacino
Scott Nicolay
Brian O'Connell
John Palisano
Christopher Roberts
Christopher Ropes
Jayaprakash Satyamurthy
Eric Schaller
Farah Rose Smith
Kim Bo Yung
Jason Zwiker

Resist and Refuse exists to benefit groups who are doing front-line work to help people who are more vulnerable than ever in our brave new post-facts world. Many different communities are at increased risk of harrassment of every sort. All proceeds from sales of *Resist and Refuse* #1 will be split into thirds and donated to Planned Parenthood, The Transgender Law Center, and The Trevor Project.

ISBN 978-0-9991430-3-2
Published by Dim Shores in August 2017

DimShores.com

 **CONTENTS**

I0683325

THIS IS NOT NORMAL

WHERE ARE WE GOING AND WHY AM I IN THIS HANDBASKET?

Hello, and thanks for picking up this first issue of *Resist and Refuse*. RAR is a new benefit zine dedicated to inclusive politics and culture, filtered through a weird literary lens. Many of our contributors come from the weird/horror fiction world, a fact which will become evident when you read the short stories.

RAR has its genesis in the brutally ugly Republican campaign for the 2016 Presidential election. U.S. elections are never pretty, but the level of open hatred on display over the last couple of years feels unprecedented. It started at the top with their nominee and filtered down to the rabid mobs of his core supporters, emboldening them to publicly say and do things that they previously felt compelled to keep to themselves. The election cycle did not create these people or their beliefs but it unquestionably made a lot of them feel comfortable with expressing their bigotry.

The Republicans' campaign slogan of "Make America great again" is not only backwards-looking but misleading. The United States has *never* been "great" for everyone. The foundations of our country were built on genocide, slavery, and exploitation. Of course, the Republicans aren't referring to those days from centuries past. Their wish is to return to a more recent time where all of these uncomfortable truths were known but could be conveniently ignored by the privileged majority of the population.

While still far, far away from a "great" society, the treatment of marginalized folks in the U.S. has made progress over the last 50 years, both legally and interpersonally. It is heartening to see so many people marching and demonstrating and speaking out. The one good thing to come out of the Republicans' shock victory is the galvanization of progressive forces. And I suspect that a large number of people are just now realizing that they, too, are progressives. When faced with the choice of going backwards to less enlightened times or continuing to move forward into the limitless future, more and more people are choosing the latter. Let's help *everyone* see the light.

— *Sam Cowan*

NON-FICTION

WE ARE THE MORAL MAJORITY

[Erin Cashier]

The Women's March on DC was utterly amazing—and it only drove home what I knew in my heart to be already true.

We are the moral majority, my friends.

Despite what portions of the nation think, we are the moral majority because we are the ones who want to build one another up, instead of crawling upon the shoulders of others as we all drown.

We are the ones who want who demand that we have affordable healthcare for everyone. That we not have pre-existing/spending caps come back. We know that people are most fulfilled in a society where they can know that no matter what happens to them, their health is cherished and protected and we will not let them down.

We are the ones who also demand that the ADA not be repealed. We are not selling our disabled brothers and sisters down the river in the name of profit.

We require educational opportunities to be available, equally, for everyone. We will not nationally privatize schools, because that is the equivalent of segregating them again. Education equals opportunity, and no where should education be more valued than in this, the land of the free.

This also means we value science, and scientists. We believe in climate change, and that the effects of it are tangible and real. We know that if the EPA is gutted we will go back to a smog-filled 70's style Silent Spring. We will not tolerate this attack on our environment it belongs to all of us, just like freedom.

We will respect our environmental stewards. We will stand strong with our brothers and sisters at Standing Rock and other places where the land itself is under attack. We will have their backs physically and financially and help them protect what is rightfully theirs.

We will also protect our black brethren. Black lives matter. Full stop. No man, woman, or child should have to walk down the street afraid a cop will shoot them down a cop that will then go free, despite video evidence showing that it was murder, clear as day. We will continue to hold our police to a higher standard, until they treat everyone equally.

We believe that mass incarceration has to end. The prison system is broken. Laws should have appropriate penalties that are metered equally, where minorities are not punished solely for the color of their skin. Prisons should be a place not of punishment, but where people can reform and then rejoin the society they belong to as fully productive members again.

Women need complete control over our own bodies. Men do not understand what it means to be un-free, what a slap in the face it feels like to have your personal autonomy be a subject up for debate. Our bodies, our lives, our decisions, end of story.

Women also need equal pay. We have labored as lesser beings, economically, for far too long. There is no reason that women should ever make less then men when they do the same work. We must fight for ourselves, and for the recognition of each other—especially our black and latina sisters who make even less than we do. We must have one another's backs and share our opportunities until all glass ceilings are shattered, everywhere, for everyone.

We will not tolerate sexism. We will no longer laugh at your rape jokes, or tell stories that denigrate others of our sex. We will hold each other and every damn last one of you accountable for the kind of 'locker talk' that puts us down in any way. We will not be made to feel lesser because of our gender, we will not listen to your cat calls as we walk by, we will not let you crush our spirits because you do not see our souls. We will never be made to feel small again. Ever.

We demand economic security. Part of this comes from education and health care, but it also comes from paying people a living wage and from appropriately taxing the rich. There is no reason why people should have secret bank accounts in the Caiman islands while fellow Americans are going hungry. We require a social safety net for all Americans, both because it is the right thing to do, and because we know that in these precarious times we are all just a feather's width away from needing it ourselves.

Our brothers and sisters from other countries, documented or not, need never hang their heads in fear. We will not be silent. There will be no registry. There will be no wall. Millions of us know you, love you, respect you, and there will be no talk of you going back. We know that our country needs you no matter your background or religion. We want you here.

We also want gay, trans, and queer people all over the gender spectrum to feel safe. We will have no truck with bathroom bills. Marriage inequality is never coming back. We will not let it. We will protect your right to healthcare as befits whatever gender you so choose. We know the strength it took for you to come out. We will never push you back again.

We will not let Nazi bullshit hurt anyone. We will stand arm in arm with our Jewish friends and call out any anti-Semitism the moment it occurs. We know that white supremacy is Nazism by another name and we know that it is evil and backwards. We will not tolerate it in our country, because it is the exact opposite of everything we stand for.

We believe that Donald Trump is an illegitimate president who won the election only with Russia's help and by playing on the most base of American fears. We will call our congresspeople every day and hold them accountable for their actions, good and bad, until his fascist authoritarian regime comes to an end.

We will protect one another with our thoughts, our words, our bodies. We know that an injustice that happens to one of us happens to all of us. We will not be broken.

That is why we're the moral majority. And that is why, when it comes to the heart and soul of America, we will win.

Come join us. We will always welcome you. ■

HOW TO WATCH A MOVIE:
A GUIDE FOR PEOPLE WHO FIND IT HARD TO TALK ABOUT OPPRESSION

[Sally Jane Black]

Scene: You and a coworker at the water cooler.
Coworker: "What did you do last night?"
You: "Oh, just watched a movie."
Coworker: "Anything good?"
You: "Let's talk about white supremacy and how it affects representations of black people in American cinema."

It might not be that simple, but it's a lot easier to bring up supposedly difficult subjects like misogyny, racism, ableism, homophobia, or any other form of oppression while living in a kyriarchy than most people think, because it's all around us, constantly. Because every facet of your life, from the clothes you wear to the systemic injustices of our laws, the only way to combat oppression is to literally be opposing in every part of your life. Some will argue that "they're just movies" (or television shows, or paintings, or comic books, or news reports, or…), but the truth is movies are a crucial part of how most Americans process the world around them. If you think back to your childhood and consider Things You Learned From Movies (etc.), you'll probably realize that there's a lot you picked up without realizing it from how people, places, and things are depicted in media and art. (The distinction between the two is often blurred, but I include both because media, in this context, refers to pervasive, accessible forms of communication and art refers to, in this context, works that have social, emotional, cultural, or political value. In most cases, these are the same thing.) Media criticism is important because media in all forms has a profound influence on us as individuals and as a society, but also because it's something almost all of us have in common: it provides us an opening for a conversation. That allows us an easier method of addressing oppression directly with others who might not otherwise ever consider it.

In order to make it easier for you, I have compiled a list of some things to consider while consuming media. This list is addressing film because that's what I feel most comfortable with, but most of these ideas can apply to almost any form of art (with a little translation effort on your part). This is written with the assumption that you are sympathetic to the idea but completely uneducated in terms of media analysis and fighting oppression. If you read this and think, "I know all this already," please, pass it along to someone you think might not. If you read this and think, "she's preaching to the choir," consider how many of your supposedly enlightened friends have done something problematic in the last week. Of course they have. We all need reminders. Which brings me to: if you read this and think, "she's said something racist, ableist, sexist, homophobic, transphobic, and/or otherwise supporting of oppression," please call me the fuck out.

STEP 1: AWARENESS

Scene: You're sitting on the couch with a couple of friends, family, strangers, fellow inmates.
Movie: [Transmisogynistic joke about how funny it is when cishet men wear dresses.]
Friends: "Oh how funny this is!"
You: "I really want to relax and enjoy this with you, but I really need to say that this is hurtful to trans women. Let me explain."

Some of the commonest complaints I get when I talk about this sort of stuff is that "they're just movies" or "I just need to turn off my brain sometimes" or "don't you ever enjoy anything?" All of these objections are bullshit.

When I was a little girl who didn't know yet that she was a girl, I watched *Ace Ventura Pet Detective*, as did many children my age. In it, a central plot point is that one character is a trans woman. When this is discovered, the titular private aye-aye reacts with overt disgust, and, in my memory (I have not rewatched since I was a child), everyone else does, too. The idea that he had kissed a trans woman—who to their minds was still a man—was so repulsive that characters vomited because of it. I recall vividly feeling horrified that my reaction to learning that the character was trans was a sort of wistful longing. I was informed forcefully by the film that I was grotesque, before I was even able to understand what I was. Moreover, the trans woman was played by a cis woman, and my reaction to this was a certain naive wonder that I had no words for beyond "Is this really possible?"

Cis actress Sean Young as a trans woman police lieutenant in *Ace Ventura, Pet Detective*. When other cops find out the character is transgender they vomit in disgust.

Ace Ventura Pet Detective was a big hit movie, Hollywood comedy schlock that most critics probably paid little heed to, one of those movies that even when the popular critics addressed it, audiences didn't much care what they had to say. It's a popcorn movie to a lot of people. It's probably now a nostalgic favorite. *Ace Ventura Pet Detective* was also probably my first direct experience with transmisogyny (that I can remember). When someone says "they're just movies," they're speaking from a place of privilege and/or ignorance, failing to consider the fact the power of representation to affect those who might not have any other sources of information. Consider also the recent hubbub over the *Ghostbusters* reboot. While the film was far from the intersectional feminist classic it should have been, the impact of seeing (cis) women in iconic roles, of seeing a straight (I think) black woman and a queer white woman in leading roles, on younger trans and cis femmes can't be denied.

Which is why you can't just turn off your brain. If you see something hurtful and laugh along with it, you're complicit. If you see something offensive in a film, then heedlessly recommend it to a friend, you've spread the offensive ideas with your tacit endorsement. If you turn off your brain, you remove yourself from the fight. Even if you see it and privately think it's bad, if you don't speak up, your silence upholds the status quo. Netflix is reading your mind. Best to let them know that and what you actually think. Yes, at first, it might feel like you're enjoying films less, but that voice telling you that opposing kyriarchy isn't fun is actually the kyriarchy's voice. Speaking out is hard work and comes with a lot of pain, but fighting for meaningful change and support is vastly more fulfilling (and therefore fun) than shrugging through the latest *Transformers* film.

The first step is just to be aware of what you are watching, to refuse to turn your brain off, to consider what you are seeing as a political statement, no matter how frivolous it seems. Forgiving something for being made by Hollywood, for coming from a source that has massive influence and reach, that is integral to a capitalist white supremacy patriarchy, is exactly the wrong way to do it. The bigger the audience, the more important it is to object.

Scene: You're watching *The Danish Girl* with a friend.
You: "As a cisgender person, this seems all right to me."
Your trans friend: "Shut the fuck up. This is garbage."

The second part of being aware of what you're watching is knowing what to look for. You don't need a film degree. You don't need to know Sembene from Spielberg. You just need to listen. If you're white, listen to people of color. If you're not disabled, listen to those who are. If you're cisgender, listen to trans people. If you're male, listen to women and non-binary people. If you're straight, listen to queer people. If you're rich, listen to people with low incomes. If you're not a sex worker, listen to sex workers. If you're not Muslim or Jewish or otherwise non-Christian, listen to Muslims and Jewish people and other non-Christian people. If you're part of a privileged group, listen to those who aren't. If you don't happen to know

anyone outside of your comfort zone, well, that's why the goddess invented social media. Follow cooking bloggers who talk about their experiences growing up poor and black. Follow agender autistic people who tweet articles about neurodiversity and video games. Follow undocumented immigrants defying silencing power structures by telling their stories and also posting pictures of their cats. Find the social media that works for you and find people to listen to.

Right now, one of you is dismissing this because social media isn't some scholarly article, but academia has always been inherently ableist, misogynistic, white supremacist, and worse, and that has silenced marginalized peoples by refusing them credibility in the eyes of the establishment and limiting their access to platforms with which to share their views. Social media has given a platform to activists of all kinds, and it's all there for you to follow. And listen.

The first step is just to be aware of what you are watching, to refuse to turn your brain off, to consider what you are seeing as a political statement, no matter how frivolous it seems.

Don't think that you are right. Don't think that you know better. Don't argue. Just listen. Once you're listening, you can watch a movie. You will never know it all. You will never be perfect. You will never be able to stop listening. But eventually, you'll be watching, and you will see something. An act of slut-shaming in *Sex and the City*. Cultural appropriation in an Andrea Arnold film. Blackface in Marx Brothers classics. Superficial representation in the latest Star Wars film. A failure at intersectionality in Kathryn Bigelow's films. A homophobic joke in an Adam Sandler flick. Something. You will see something wrong, and you will have enough understanding to say something.

You'll also probably want to say something. So do so. Tell the person watching with you. Tell your coworker the next day. Tell the next person who asks you about what movies you like. Tell the next person you pass on the streets. Tell your Uber driver. Tell your parole officer. Tell your problematic cousin. Tell your mom. Tell your drug dealer. Tell your favorite communist Facebook group. Tell your blog. Hell, just tell it to Twitter. We live in an era where you need no excuse to say anything, because social media has made sharing your thoughts on anything normal. Think about the last time you Instagrammed your breakfast and ask yourself whether that's any more or less worthy of being shared than your thoughts on why *Citizen Kane* is a big misogynistic mess (hint: they are of equal importance). More importantly, remember that movies are small talk. People use them all the time in casual conversation; it's an opportunity for you to turn fighting oppression into a natural part of small talk. It's an opportunity to turn small talk into big talk. It's an opportunity to normalize resistance.

STEP 2: ANALYSIS (STYLE IS SUBSTANCE)

Scene: You are watching *Guardians of the Galaxy*.

Your chauvinist cishet male acquaintance: "That actress is so fucking hot."

You: "The cinematography of this is focused overtly on the actresses' bodies in an uncomfortable manner that suggests this film is objectifying women intentionally."

The majority of people seem to respond to films almost solely on the basis of their plots. You can see this in almost every response to a film: someone tells you what they liked about a movie and their response is a synopsis. Someone talks about that awesome moment where Tom Cruise repelled down a building to get the secret whatever, or how good it felt to see Tim Robbins glory in muddy rainfall after escaping prison not because of how it looked or how it sounded, but because of how it served the plot: he escaped prison! People know that the music and the camera angle and the lighting matter for how it makes them feel, but they either just don't talk about it or they don't necessarily get why or how. Or maybe they just don't think about it.

And you don't have to, either. You don't need to know that shooting from a slightly low angle makes people seem bigger and thus more powerful on screen. You don't need to know what a dolly zoom is. You don't need to understand J-cuts. You don't need to get into the details of color filters and what kind of camera and film was used… if you don't want to. All of that can and should matter, depending on how it's used, but it's not necessary to always seeing how a story is told. Anyone can watch a film and understand where the camera is looking. Anyone can watch a film and notice who the camera is looking at. Anyone can watch a film and pay attention to who has more lines, who is the butt of the jokes, how many times the camera shows someone's reactions, when the camera is showing someone or something. You don't have to think of these things in terms of lenses, cuts, focuses, or angles. You just need to think of it as what you are being shown and told.

You know what it looks and sounds like when a movie is trying to tell you someone is sexy. You probably don't even think about it, but you also probably immediately thought of something when I said that. Think as you watch films who they are treating this way. Is it always cishet white women? It usually is. Are they ever disabled? Almost never. When black women are treated this way, is it different somehow than when white women are? (Hint: Often, yes.) Now consider the last time you saw a fat woman treated this way by a film. Was it intended to entice you, or to make you laugh? It's easy to tell from context without any knowledge of film theory or technical details. You've seen this your whole life. When the film goes out of its way to inform the viewer that a character is sexy, what qualities of that person is it emphasizing? Have you ever seen a film that successfully conveys sexual attractiveness without emphasizing a certain body type?

This sort of analysis can apply to pretty much anything. Simple compare-and-contrast can reveal a lot about a film.

Who in the film is shown to have more agency? Who gets more things done, pushes the plot along actively? Take *Snow White* and take *Tangled*: how is Snow White's role different from Rapunzel's? Who is in control of the plot? Who has to be saved by a man? Who faces her own evil parental figure on her own? Consider how the white buddy cop hero of your favorite action film is shown vs. how the black buddy cop hero of your favorite action film. Who is given the better lines? Who is given the big hero moment at the end? Who is shown to be right the whole time? These are some of the simpler questions to ask, but they will only lead you deeper. Why is Tom Cruise the hero and not Paula Patton? (If your answer is that Tom Cruise is a bigger box office draw, then ask yourself why that is.) Are there any people of color at all in *Donnie Darko*? In *Fight Club*? How are they treated by the film? Who has more lines, more importance to the plot, more character development?

Tangled's main character Rapunzel has agency and doesn't rely on the prince to save her.

This sort of analysis is never more important than in analyzing films claiming to be anti-oppression. *Django Unchained* is a direct look at racism and makes it very explicit. Unless you are an outright Nazi, you probably won't walk away from that film with sympathies toward slave owners. However, Tarantino and his crew employ a hyper-violent style in many of the scenes of conflict in the film that permeates even non-gunfight moments, leading to moments where the camera lingers on black suffering. Because the film seems to relish violence by making it cartoonish (notice how the blood sprays in the big shootout at the mansion, notice how the film uses a sudden death at the dinner table to shock the audience for cheap thrills), the scenes of black people being physically harmed are set in a similar context. It makes what could be a powerful statement feel like cheap exploitation. The film indulges in racist behavior—perhaps relatively subtle compared to the slavery it attempts to directly object to, but only relatively—while denouncing racism, sending the message that superficial resistance is acceptable. It satisfies a need to feel like you are fighting racism while not actually doing a damned thing about it.

For an older example, consider Stanley Kubrick's antiwar efforts. In *Full Metal Jacket*, the manner in which the Viet Cong sniper dies is slow and sadistic. She suffers on the ground, begging for death, while white soldiers argue over the morality of showing her mercy. This is used as a message about war, but rather than depicting the sniper woman with any humanity, she is a prop to humanize the moral struggles of the American soldiers. The film lingers on her, lying on the ground, twitching, while showing the soldiers above her. It conveys a message about violence and war, but it does so by using her pain, not empathizing with it. Meanwhile, in *Paths of Glory*, the predominantly white cast of characters are shown with equal sympathy, and the unjust deaths shown are done in a manner that still respected the victims—in fact, in a way that showed more respect for the victims than almost anyone else. Their pain is used to drive home much the same message, but no one is used as a prop.

It matters how they tell the story. The style is the film's substance. It conveys an idea as much as the plot does. Paying attention, even to simple things like who is shown in close up and when or to how long the camera watches something can give you an idea of underlying attitudes present in the filmmaking.

Scene: You and a friend watch *Lawrence of Arabia*.
Friend: "Now I really want to visit the Middle East."
You: "You know, it's not just one big desert."

Understanding that how a film shows something is significant is one of the main ways to understand how setting affects the themes of a film. Blatant examples abound of films using non-Western, non-white locations as "exotic." Look at how the *Pirates of the Caribbean* movies treat Singapore and notice the stereotypes there. Look at how *Crocodile Dundee* treats gay bars. Look at how a film views Wall Street, the White House, or the condos of the rich vs. how it views the Pyramids, the seat of Venezuela's government, or the homes of the poor. Is your favorite war movie showing Vietnam as a place where people are fighting against colonization and capitalism, or is it showing American soldiers killing faceless Viet Cong soldiers who kill babies?

An analysis of characters in any film is probably the quickest way to perceive its biases. For the most part, any character that is a member of a marginalized group is probably going to be a stereotype in any given Hollywood film—and most indie films in America and other capitalist countries. Be on the look out for Asian characters with mystical powers and martial arts skills, blind people who are see more without their eyes, black women who are sassy instead of having any other personality trait, Muslim fathers who are too controlling, trans women who are sex workers, sex workers with hearts of gold who just need saving, sexless fat people who serve as punchlines, gay best friends, dead lesbians, LatinX people whose accents are exaggerated for the sake of comedy, people with disabilities who serve as inspiration for able-bodied people, autistic people with psychic abilities… Anything that fetishizes marginalized people, turns us into punchlines, or leaves us as a standard token representative is dehumanizing, humiliating, and oppressive.

All of this is in build up to the most important part, which is what ideas and themes the film presents. Most stories boil down to a few tired ideas of good and evil or love or something

> *Anything that fetishizes marginalized people, turns us into punchlines, or leaves us as a standard token representative is dehumanizing, humiliating, and oppressive.*

like that, but what they present as good, evil, or love is what matters. In *Star Wars* (to use the simplest possible example), evil is based on fascism, and calling the enemy an "empire" certainly has implications. It's basic. Analysis of the characters and the setting can reveal problems in how the films treat women and people of color, however, and how these tie into its view of good/evil make it more complicated. Jabba the Hut objectifies Leia in a disgusting manner, but the film's fans have fetishized that outfit in a way that is certainly contextual evidence that *Return of the Jedi* does not effectively present Jabba's patriarchal enslavement of her as problematic enough. Evil is often presented as physically disabled, elderly, and selfish. The good guys include a roguish individual who pushes himself on a woman. Each of those things has a different impact on the theme of good and evil and the ideas the film sends.

Films with more complex themes obviously require engagement as well, but not necessarily more "intellectual" engagement. The first time you use a popcorn movie to talk about anything deeper than how cool the explosions are, you're bound to meet someone who complains that you're reading too much into it. Fuck that person. Popcorn movies are seen by more people than art films, and therefore, demand vigorous analysis—they're what's speaking to our children and friends and enemies and represent a lot of what rich people think we want to think. Discussing Barbara Hammer's approach to feminism and how her very biological focus may or may not be excluding trans people—it's an essay that I'd love to read or a discussion I'd love to engage—but telling people how racist [insert blockbuster here] is is important, too.

STEP 3: CONTEXT

Scene: Your house next to your DVD collection.
You: *throws away everything Woody Allen ever had anything to do with.*

Who directed the film? A woman of color or a white man? A black trans queer woman or a LatinX straight non-binary person? It matters. It sets a tone by virtue of informing the voice of the film, but also, it shows you how the film fits into the oppressive systems of the world. That context can provide insights into the film—from rather directly informing the film's meaning, such as all those films about Woody Allen objectifying and trying to have sex with younger women, to more removed contexts like Oscar Michieaux's works as a black filmmaker in the 1920s somehow getting films made despite violent racism all around him making every film of his seem like a miracle. There is a myth that you need to be objective and judge a film only by its technical merits, but those technical merits have been defined through history by ruling class white cis men. Every rule in the book has been broken by filmmakers who are credited with being revolutionary and upheld by the critics and public alike for being innovative while at the same time, works by filmmakers who aren't white cishet able-bodied neurotypical men (or some combination of those that usually includes "white" and "men" more than anything else) are disregarded. Those films by, say, black filmmakers that reach critical acceptance or public approval despite breaking a few rules usually are done either by filmmakers who have proven their ability to meet kyriarchal standards or combine technical craft that meets those standards with those that don't.

Or, in other words, Spike Lee might make challenging, thought-provoking, essential cinema, but the reason he is more well known and lauded than Hailie Gerima is because he makes films that meet a certain standard long defined by white people. Gerima's films—which are more experimental and sometimes rooted in other storytelling techniques—are just as good if not better than Lee's films (depends on the film, but *Bush Mama* and *Malcolm X* are essential cinema for everyone). This is not to say that Lee's films are diluted somehow or that Lee hasn't faced racist rejections—quite the contrary, there is a long and important history in art in reclamation and Lee has faced significant discrimination in his career as well—but simply that the way his films are judged is rooted in white supremacist values. He is open about his love of cinema history and his craft shows it. Watching a movie and judging it solely on technical craft concedes to those standards. What matters isn't whether a film meets those standards, but whether the film makes a point worth hearing, evokes a feeling worth feeling, creates an idea worth creating. How it does that matters only insofar as its effectiveness. While, granted, all white people in America are products of and informed by a white supremacist society— and therefore, art created to white supremacist standards might be more effective at reaching us because that's all we can understand—it's crucial to our breaking those standards for us to become aware of them and stop using them. While it is impossible for me to understand what it is to experience being black, it is possible for me to understand what it means to be white and actively deconstruct that until I am no longer confused, disoriented, or offended by things rooted in different standards. If I watch enough films by black filmmakers, I'll begin to pick up on patterns, find unexpected familiarities, and though I will not fully understand the experience of being black, I will begin to wither the white supremacist filter that inevitably infests my viewpoint.

Context is a very contentious aspect of engaging with film. Many people will argue that you should separate art from the artist, and to some extent, everyone does this. But there's nothing wrong with not doing it, and often times, it's necessary

A scene from Hailie Gerima's critically lauded *Bush Mama*, shot as his thesis film at UCLA.

to speaking out against oppression and violence. Woody Allen is an easy target, and so is Bill Cosby, but many, many filmmakers are deeply problematic. Kubrick and Hitchcock were known for mistreating actresses "in the name of art" to get the performances they wanted. Werner Herzog's approach to *Fitzcarraldo* seems a bit fucked up to say the least in regards to how the indigenous people were endangered by his grandiose re-creation. Bertolucci admits he and Marlon Brando conspired to sexually assault Maria Schneider for the sake of performance, and Dusan Makavejev did a lot of fucked up things in *Sweet Movie*. A lot of men in Hollywood have been accused of sexual assault or harassment, a lot of your favorite white filmmakers and performers have said some racist bullshit, and any cisgender performer who plays a transgender person is guilty of heavy transphobia. Like their movies or not, but if you're going to talk about their work, it's a good time to talk about why what they did or do or said or whatever was wrong.

On the flipside, we have films like *Madchen in Uniform*, a queer film made in 1931 in Germany. We have Oscar Michieaux making films about and for black people before the Civil Rights Movement hit the national stage. Jack Smith, Kenneth Anger, and many other directors were openly, unapologetically gay before that was even remotely safe. Cheryl Dunye made the first black lesbian feature length film in the early 90s (yes, it took that long, as far as we know), and Eva Robin's had a role in *Tenebrae* back in 1982. The improbability of these films being made back then (or even now) is so great that their existence is something of a wonder. They deserve credit for that.

It's also important to understand that films by and for oppressed peoples have existed almost as long as films have. Queer films (and directors), sexually progressive films, and films by women in general have often been ignored by history, but these all existed in abundance before the Hays Code of 1933. So many early silent films have been lost that it's impossible to really know what film content was like in the early days, but especially in the early 1930s, there were a lot of more risqué films to be seen. Many of these might seem tame by today's standards, but their place in film history and their role in giving queer people some semblance of representation can't be understated.

Scene: You are looking through your DVDs.
You: "Let's watch some foreign cinema."
Your friend: "Oh, cool. Do you have anything from Africa?"
You: "There are lots of countries and cultures in Africa. Let's watch Sambizanga. It's from Angola."

This one's easy: if your favorite movies are all white, all heterosexual, all cisgender, all American, all Anglophonic, all male-centric, all neurotypical, all able-bodied, all Christian, all capitalist, or all Francis Ford Coppola, if your entire DVD collection are films you can find at the top of the highest grossing lists, most likely, you need to dig a little. Drop every assumption you have about what some place or person or thing is like, and start watching new kinds of films. You might have to look outside of Netflix! That said, Netflix does have LGBTQIA+ categories (they limit it to LGBT, but they do include intersex films in there! I have not yet found an explicitly asexual film), even if a lot of them are probably not the best choices. You can still find *Tangerine* there (as of this writing), though, and that's a fucking masterpiece. Same with *Pariah*.

© 2015 Magnolia Pictures

L-R: Transgender actresses Mya Taylor and Kitana Kiki Rodriguez in *Tangerine*.

There are lists all over the Internet of films by African-American directors, films by women (directors, editors, and writers!), queer films, trans films, films about people with disabilities, "foreign language" (read: non-English—listed here in colonialist phrasing because that's how to find it easiest if you are searching for it) films, and so on. If you've questions about a film's portrayal, listen to those it portrays. *Moonlight* was lauded by queer black men (see Robert Jones' review in Essence); Tyler Perry is denounced by them. Trans women hated *The Crying Game*. White queer trans women can't speak to the cultural experiences of those they are not, so take these recommendations with a grain of salt. Don't trust this piece—

go find out for yourself. See not just whether people liked films or not, but why—is *Selena* apparently beloved by Mexican-Americans because it accurately reflects their experiences? It shouldn't take too much searching to find out.

Maybe right now you are thinking, "But I can't just watch something because a black person made it! That's racist!"

Then don't do that! Watch things that black people made that sound interesting to you for other reasons, but be sure to examine what the reasons you like something are. If you're not watching something because a black person made it, that's definitely racist. Decolonize your tastes. Take time to focus on things you might not otherwise watch. Promote things you like that aren't part of the kyriarchy's canon of *The Godfather*, *Gone With the Wind*, and *Interstellar*. If you find a South American indigenous film, tell people about it and share it. If you discover a Senegalese masterpiece, invite friends over to watch and talk about it. Remember that loving and sharing is great, but calling it your own is problematic. Appreciate, don't appropriate.

By now you're fucking exhausted and everything you loved has turned to dust, but there's good news. Just because you're pushing your boundaries doesn't mean you have to let go of everything you once loved. Re-examine them, certainly, and ask yourself: why do you love them? It's perfectly acceptable if the answer is "they brought me joy when I was younger" or "I relate to the characters" (assuming you aren't relating to them because they're white supremacists or something). But if you can't find an easy answer, or if your answer is problematic, then maybe distance yourself from it or find a new way to love it.

There is a long tradition of queer and trans reading of ostensibly straight or cis media. Documentaries like *The Celluloid Closet* cover this in detail, but in short, qualities we find familiar in characters presented as straight or cis are taken as subtle indications of being queer and/or trans. The relationship depicted in *Calamity Jane* or Rock Hudson's career stand out as generally accessible examples. This method of reading films can be applied in other ways. Many neurodivergent people apply a similar tactic in finding characters whose experiences with, say, borderline personality is reflected in how they are portrayed but non-explicit. This can also apply to reading a film from a feminist perspective, finding subtle cues of empowerment or simple joy in defied expectations. You might find it unlikely that *Long Island Cannibal Massacre's* scene where a woman is run over by a lawnmower could be effectively argued to be about the human struggle with the idea of wilderness vs. civilization, but one of the best film reviews I've ever read made this argument poetically. Treasure can be found in the worst muck.

What's most important about this is that it is a method of combating the effects of erasure (in the form of a lack of representation). Almost all oppression takes the form of erasure, with genocide being the ultimate form to hate-speech being a form of reduction and silencing that effectively erases people. Treasure hunting/queer reading/trans reading finds representation hidden in things not made for us. It's reclamation, demanding representation where we ought to have been. Sharing these ideas spreads—slowly, quietly—the idea that we have always been here and always will be here. Pulling older films out of darkness and obscurity has a similar effect, arguably more palpably so.

When engaging older media, though, do not concede to the standards of the past. Being made in 1919 does not excuse racism in film; being made in Nazi Germany doesn't excuse being Nazi propaganda. *Triumph of the Will* is a piece of shit movie and no one should say anything nice about it, ever. Let go of the idea of something being a "product of its time." People engage older media all the time, and it deserves to be understood through your own perspective and not the perspective of the white patriarchs of the past. Nothing "makes up for" problems in a film, either. You can like a film with flaws in it; admitting those flaws exist doesn't make it a bad film or you a bad person. Admitting those flaws exist is a gateway to communicating what those flaws mean—especially when those flaws are forms of or symptoms of oppression.

STEP 4: SELF-CARE

Scene: You've just come home from throwing bricks at a Starbucks and feeding rich people to hungry communist revolutionaries.
You: "Time to relax! Let's put on Moana!"

Don't burn yourself out. If you need something that brings you joy, watch something that brings you joy. If I ever need to cry, I will put on *Little Women* and bawl my fucking eyes out. Find the things that work for you and bring you healing. This is not to say that you should turn your brain off, but rather, redirect it toward comfort and care. Engage with art that heals you and examine why and seek more like it. You know yourself and your needs better than others, so I won't go into too much detail here. Just be well, my loves.

STEP 5: COMMUNICATION

Finally.

The hard part.

The benefit of using art and media as a gateway to these discussions is that it can (that is, has the possibility of but not the certainty of) provide a buffer. While people are often passionate about films they love, they are even more sensitive about being called a racist. Sometimes, though, if you call their favorite movie racist, maybe they'll listen.

It doesn't happen often.

This isn't about reaching right wing folks. This isn't about reaching Nazis. There's a line that's hard to pinpoint between people to engage with debate and people to just punch in the face. We all have different standards (I'd say to the right of Trotsky is a waste of time, but here I am, talking to people I can't even guess at the politics of), but more or less my target audience is Democrats and liberals, white feminists, and other non-intersectional, non-communist (adjust to anarchist or other leftist position as suits your needs, I suppose) leftists. This is about reaching the 60 million people who voted for Hillary and the slightly (only very slightly) smaller percentage of them who actually thought she'd change things for the better instead of maintaining a destructive, oppressive status quo. This is for those who attended the Women's March and wore pussy hats and took pictures of the indigenous protestor's religious ceremonies and didn't understand why it was wrong to pose in wheelchairs when they didn't need wheelchairs. This is for the people whose road to reinforcing the Hell we live in is paved with the good intentions of resisting it, but don't realize they're still part of the kyriarchy's machinery.

You know who at your water cooler is sympathetic. You know which of your friends can be reached. You know best how to argue with your cousin, your dad, your brother, your great uncle. Analyzing art is important and critics and creators alike have a responsibility to call out problematic works, but anyone, literally anyone, can and will talk about movies, tv shows, books, comics, radio jingles, tissue paper brand mascots, and ancient cave drawings, and if you're not comfortable bringing up resisting white supremacy without some sort of prompt, well, these provide your opportunity. Test the waters and start putting yourself out there. Draw from personal experience and from what you've read and learned. Keep reading and learning. Keep seeking new things. Share new things. "Oh you liked *Pariah*? Have you seen *The Watermelon Woman*?" "No, I don't think *Religulous* is a good film. Let's talk about Islamophobia, Bill Maher, and ableism."

Silliness aside, it's not easy to assert your opinion, but sliding these things into casual conversation about media and art can help create natural segues into bigger issues. It's not a replacement for direct action, creating safe spaces, challenging bigoted policies in your work space, protecting those who are most affected by oppression (with your body if necessary), and violently resisting the rise of fascism, but it's a step in making resistance part of every facet of your life. It's not just getting offended and boycotting the obvious bullshit like Adam Sandler movies. It's not just reading the work of trans poets and black revolutionaries and neurodivergent lawyers. It's letting it into literally everything you do, from grocery shopping to driving your car to watching television or reading articles online. It's not easy—I certainly haven't achieved it, either—but when white supremacy, patriarchy, and capitalism are pervasive throughout our lives, so must be our resistance to them. You've made it part of your life already if you're reading this. You're supporting some organization, you're out in the streets, you're making your own social media posts, you're sharing all the right memes, you're speaking up at work at home at school, but it's never enough. (I bet you feel that way a lot. I know I do.) Until we're all making every facet of our lives an act of resistance, we're not adequately resisting. Everything we do requires a new way of looking at it.

And also read *Settlers: The Mythology of the White Proletariat* by J Sakai. ■

ALTERNATIVE FACTS: TRUMPISM IN MY SCHOOL

[Brian O'Connell]

In discussing the effect of the Trump administration on some of my peers, I am reminded of The The's song "The Beat(en) Generation", which discusses how the most recent wave of children has been affected by the sociopolitical climate: being told that "freedom lives in the barrels of a warm gun", being "reared on a diet of prejudice and misinformation", &c. In the song, the narrator implores the titular generation to "open their eyes…[and] imagination". I believe that if such a thing is going to occur, it has been severely set back by the election of the demagogue who now tweets from the White House.

I'm a ninth grader in a suburban town, mostly white, that has consistently voted democratic for the past few years. It has a low crime rate, good schools, and is generally quite nice. Unfortunately, the Trump election has stirred up a lot of the youth in the town, and in particularly unsettling ways.

In my younger brother's school (he's in eighth grade), a mock presidential election was held to see the school's general opinion. Trump won by ten points or so. I was outside, waiting to pick my brother up, when this was announced, and it was greeted with overwhelming cheers from the kids and some very troubled expressions from the adults. Whether or not these kids were simply voting for Trump because they thought he was funny (possible) or actually rooting for his bigoted ideals (also possible) is unclear. What I can say is that my brother recently saw a fellow student shouting at some poor kid "You got a problem with Trump, bro?" in the hallway.

In my school things are much palpably worse. On the day after election day, a black girl rather meekly muttered that she was uncomfortable with the election to a white friend of hers. This friend immediately started shouting "You'd rather have a criminal in office?" until the girl quietly apologized.

A Mexican student was talking with his friends and said that he feared Trump. His friends immediately started to tease him (in an admittedly normal way for boys of this age), saying that he was going to be deported. The Mexican student simply replied that he was an American and that he felt like it was the end of the world.

I bring these examples up—and they're not the worst of them, believe me—simply to exhibit that, in some predominantly white friend groups, marginalized students are either a) not allowed to express their opinion or b) not able to have their opinion fully appreciated. This contributes to a lack of healthy discourse between groups.

I'd rather it be this, though, than the bullying, which is also occurring (and in pretty awful ways). The students most targeted in these instances are black, female, and gay teens. I've seen them get shoved in the hallways, teased by older students, and frequently yelled at by peers.

I myself was bullied by two people during and after the election, and while I'll not get into the nitty-gritty of the reasons why they bullied me (things got quite personal), I was treated to the following lectures:

- how if Trump didn't win it would be "revolution" (after the election they said that they'd be "upset" if Hillary won, but not "whiny")
- why "feminists are stupid"
- how Clinton had "admitted to rigging the election" (I did some research into this – the only thing I found was an article about a 2006 tape in which Clinton allegedly said it might be beneficial for the U.S. to keep an eye on the Iraq election, which I haven't confirmed)
- how the Holocaust didn't happen (even though one of them was descended from a Nazi)
- why it doesn't matter that Putin arranged the murder of a British reporter (answer: because he's British)
- how they'd actually tried to join the KKK
- how Trump should have Muslims and immigrants (including children) shot
- how they took advantage of a Mexican special needs kid who didn't know better
- why the word "n-gger" should be back in the dictionary
- why "n-ggers" couldn't swim
- how they could be friends with black people but not be in a relationship with them or let them into their houses
- how my brother is "weak," my friends are "awful," and my loved ones are "stupid"
- how I'm "terrible"
- how they'd "literally kill me" if I ever told on them

Their love of Trump bordered on hero worship, as if he was some sort of messiah (which is certainly how he's styling himself) and they freely admit that they're racist (and then pride themselves for being "honest"). They also insulted my friends but then play nice in front of them (to the point where a few of those insulted are actually friendly with them).

I kind of pity kids like this in an awful way. They're products of their parents, who are evidently just as bigoted and awful as they are. You don't choose who raises you.

I know opinions change and that they might regret all of this later in life, but the fact that Trump is going to be president during those formative years is going to set back (or eliminate) that important development of empathy. Same goes for… anyone under twenty, really.

I would suggest – no, plead - that any parents reading this talk to their children openly about issues like racism, misogyny, homophobia, and so on. It'll really, really help them later in life – that is, if Betsy DeVos hasn't irreparably screwed up the education system by then.

Scary times. ■

APOLOGY, REDIRECTED

[Rebecca J. Allred]

I feel the need to apologize, because what I'm about to say may make some readers uncomfortable. This is not an unusual state of being for me; I am—by nature and by nurture—a nonconfrontational person. I have learned that it is infinitely easier to shoulder discomfort than to try and resolve it, because the pursuit of resolution is rife with opportunities to compound an already significant distress. I've learned that my reactions to negative stimuli are based on emotion, that my emotions—by default of my gender—are irrational at best, hyperbolic at worst, and, as a result, should be kept to myself.

What follows is a list of anecdotes. The most memorable craters left behind after traversing the misogynistic minefield that I and so many others are forced to negotiate on a daily basis. None of these stories is new. My experiences are not unique. The only thing that makes these encounters remarkable is how unremarkable they are. They are an expression of the status quo. An unacceptable reality that we're all supposed to silently accept because that's the way it is. Move along. Nothing to see here…

I'm seven or eight years old when the neighbor boy ushers me into a dark closet and asks me to remove articles of my clothing. He's a kid too—not an adult—so it never occurs to me that I am in danger. Never occurs to me that something bad is about to happen. Something I will force myself to forget until more than a decade later when a passing comment unearths the memory—sharp and vivid and so completely unexpected that I question whether or not it really happened. But of course it did.

When it's over, I don't feel that I've done anything wrong until he warns me not to talk about it. That if I do, my dad won't love me anymore, because: "You're dirty now."

Even after I remember and am able to evaluate the situation through the eyes of an adult, it takes me a long time to fully appreciate the words he chose to cage me. He didn't threaten me with disapproval from my mother or my sister, my friends or my teachers. He didn't even threaten me with physical harm. He tells me that if anyone finds out about what I have done, my father—the patriarch, law-maker, and ultimate authority figure—will be the one to punish me by withholding his love and approval.

The threat is effective.

I'm twelve, and I go out to dinner with my grandmother, one of her friends, and a group of kids comprised of both sets of grandchildren. The restaurant has a pool table. I've never played pool before, but it looks fun, so I ask if anyone would be willing to show me how. One of the other women's grandsons is a bit older, maybe 14, and he offers to teach me.

We're at the table less than five minutes when a woman unrelated to our group steps up and informs us that pool is a man's game. That ladies would never play such a game—only

women with loose morals. She says if I play my cards right and behave like a lady, one day I'll make the boy a good wife. Then, as if it's a complement: "Just look at those birthing hips!"

The boy is visibly embarrassed, so I apologize and return to the table. Because that's what women do—apologize for making men uncomfortable.

I'm fifteen, sitting in Trig/Algebra II, and the boy sitting in front of me turns around to ask if I'll help him with his homework. Another boy leans across the aisle and asks, "Why would you want her help? She doesn't even have a nice rack."

Later, I ask the first boy if he still wants my help. Despite the fact that I consistently put up one of the top scores in the class, he says, "No, thanks."

> She says if I play my cards right and behave like a lady, one day I'll make the boy a good wife. Then, as if it's a complement: "Just look at those birthing hips!" The boy is visibly embarrassed, so I apologize and return to the table. Because that's what women do — apologize for making men uncomfortable.

I'm sixteen, and I ask for power tools for Christmas so I can use them to build sets in my theatre production class. I get jewelry instead.

I'm eighteen. A freshman in college majoring in theatre. One night, as my classmates and I wait back stage, one of the boys makes a series of rude and unwelcome comments/suggestions toward me. I do what I've done in similar situations dozens of times before. I ignore him. I ignore him up until the moment he puts his hands on me, until he pushes me up against the wall and licks the side of my face. He does this in full view of the other students. My friends. The boys laugh. So do some of the girls. Nobody says or does anything to make it stop. So I laugh, too. Because if I laugh, maybe this will be the end of it. This time, it is.

I'm nineteen. A sophomore in college majoring in biological science. A friend comes up to me and says, "The funniest thing just happened. You won't believe it!"

She says: "You know those two guys who sit up in the corner. One of them just cornered me in the cafeteria and told me that I need to make you wear a bra because you're making his friend uncomfortable."

His married-with-two-kids friend... His deeply religious friend...

I look at what I am wearing. Jeans and a modest tank—100% opaque. And, no, I'm not wearing a bra, because they're goddamn uncomfortable and I don't like wearing them, but I'm small-breasted enough that you can't really tell unless you're looking closely.

I'm twenty-one and deep in my pre-requisite studies for medical school. My regular study group is comprised of myself and two other students, one male and one female. The woman is a friend of mine and we've been studying together for the better part of a year. This is the first class we've shared with the man, but he's smart and fun and wants to be a doctor just like we do.

One night about a week before an exam we make plans to study at his place. I'm running late and before I step out, my friend calls and tells me not to come. She sounds weird, but she's got a lot going on in her life; she always sounds a little weird. I assume its unrelated to the study group and figure if it's important, we'll talk about it later.

And we do.

She tells me that she arrived early and while they were alone, our study partner had raped her. She tells me that when it was over, when she was collecting her things and crying, his only comment was: "I should have waited for Rebecca."

Later, when she confesses to a person in a position of authority, they advise her to "chalk it up to biological experience. Rapists don't go to jail."

I don't know if that man ever became a doctor, but I do know that there's nothing in the preceding account that would prevent him from becoming president.

I'm twenty-two, preparing to have emergency surgery. The doctor in the emergency room asks me if there's any chance I could be pregnant. I tell him no.

"No sex?" he asks.

"No," I answer.

He pats me on the head and says, "Good girl."

I'm twenty-four. My fiancé tells me the cost of my birth control (which I pay for myself) is wasted, because I don't put out enough to justify the expense.

I'm twenty-five and working at my first post-college job. A male coworker discusses his plans to ask for a raise and casually mentions his current rate. It's $5.00/hour higher than I'm being compensated, despite the fact that I've worked for the company longer and that his prior experience is on par with my own.

I ask my employers for an assessment of my performance, and when it's confirmed that my work is more than satisfactory, I ask for a merit-based raise. My request is denied.

Not long after that, I overhear another conversation. This time, the same male colleague is talking about how great it is to work for a company that values its contractors and doesn't mind spending money to keep the good ones around. It isn't until I start applying for other jobs that I'm offered an incentive-based raise; even then, it's still less than my male colleague's pre-raise rate.

I'm twenty-five and a first year medical student. I'm sitting in class—a class I'm already paying interest on that is supposed

I stayed quiet because I didn't think people would believe me. Because if they did believe me, they'd say it was my fault. Or that it wasn't a big deal. Or that I should stop complaining because others have it worse.

to be teaching me the foundations of medicine. Instead, I'm clenching fists beneath my desk as a male instructor laments the non-discriminatory policies that do a disservice to the field of medicine.

He says: "Women are much better applicants, but they make poor doctors."

He says: "Admissions boards should be able to take an applicant's reproductive plans into consideration when deciding whether or not to admit her to medical school."

I'm twenty-five. Twenty-six. Twenty-seven... I'm on the wards. I'm treating patients. I have this conversation over and over and over again...

"Are you the nurse?"

"Actually, I'm a medical student."

"So you're studying to become a nurse?"

"No. I'm studying to become a doctor."

"Really? Huh. What does your husband think about that?"

"I'm not married."

"Of course you're not."

Some of these stories I've told more times that I can count. Others I've never confessed until now. Why? There are so many reasons, but like the stories above, none of them are unique. I stayed quiet because I didn't think people would believe me. Because if they did believe me, they'd say it was my fault. Or that it wasn't a big deal. Or that I should stop complaining because others have it worse. Because people watched it happen and still didn't do anything to help. But the biggest reason is because I've learned that the most important thing in life for a woman is to get along—especially with men. Because if you don't, you're going to be punished.

I'm thirty-five. Donald Trump is the Republican nominee for the 2016 presidential election. I needn't remind you of the countless questionable and unquestionably offensive things that he says and does. I stare into the glow of my computer screen, watching it unfold like a poorly-written dystopian film.

When I cast my vote, I'm thinking about these things that have happened to me. I'm also thinking about what sorts of things—worse things, unspeakable things—might happen to someone else if a man who openly mocks the disabled, a man who recommends a registry based on religious affiliation, a man who not only admits to but boasts about his own sexually predatory behavior is elected President of the United States. I don't vote for myself, because even though I've felt the tremors of inequality, I am still so very privileged. I fear for myself, yes, but I fear more for the thousands of Americans who do not share my position of relative safety.

I'm thirty-six, and I watch in numb horror as #45 postures; as the tsunami of hate and destruction engulfs the country; as irreparable damage is done in the course of less than a week and the United States begins to unravel at the seams. I'm called a poor loser. A snowflake. A politically correct crybaby. I'm told to stop fighting. To lie down and just accept what's happening. Because I'm a woman, and at the end of the day, this is what I deserve. I have nobody to blame but myself.

But my experiences are symptoms of a much more insidious disease, and while I've been blindly focused on alleviating them, I've passively ignored the underlying malignancy that's been growing and metastasizing since before I was born. In a sense, I suppose it is my fault. I didn't speak up. Not for myself and not for anyone else.

I began writing this with the promise of an apology on my lips—a mea culpa for making some readers uncomfortable—but as I draw to a close, I've realized that I'm not sorry anymore. Not for the reasons I'm used to. You should be uncomfortable. And so should I. We should all be in a state of agony over the combined missteps that have led us to where we are today. From now on, I reserve my apologies for the victims, not the perpetrators, of discrimination and injustice.

I'm sorry. I'm sorry that preserving my personal comfort was more important than putting an end to systematic suffering. I'm sorry I wasn't a better listener. I'm sorry I wasn't a better ally. I'm sorry I stood idle for so long, and in so doing, benefitted from that idleness. I'm sorry I didn't do more to stop this from happening.

I'm not asking for forgiveness. I am owed precisely what I've offered up to this point, and that is exactly nothing. What I'm asking for is an opportunity to help make things right. To finally add my voice and use my privilege to the benefit of others instead of just myself. To create an apology that is more than mere words but actions that actually mean something. To speak up when others are silenced, and to listen when it is not my turn to speak. I will stumble, and I will make mistakes, and when I do, I will learn what I can, but I will not shrink back into my corner of shame. I will not continue to hide in the safety of others' oppression.

I'm thirty-six, and I'm sorry, but being sorry never fixed anything that was broken. ∎

Photograph by Bonzo McGrue, San Diego, CA

SELENA CHAMBERS AND FARAH ROSE SMITH IN CONVERSATION

[Selena Chambers, Farah Rose Smith]

The following is a discussion held throughout February 2017 between editrixes and writers Selena Chambers and Farah Rose Smith.

Selena Chambers is the founder and editor-in-chief of *Nasty Writers*, a quarterly, crossed-genre, literary magazine showcasing women writers with a particularly "nasty" bent. It's mission is two-fold: 1) To dedicate a space for the preservation and exploration of the radical intersections between feminism, art, and literature, including discussions about race, gender, sexuality, and disability within a national and international context. 2) To focus on the pivotal, symbiotic tradition of writing as a form for female resistance, and honor how important writing has been to Feminism, especially when it was one of the few avenues a woman could utilize for financial independence.

In addition to editing, her fiction and non-fiction have appeared in a variety of venues including *Mungbeing* magazine, *Clarkesworld*, *The Non-Binary Review*, *Tor.com*, *Bookslut*, and in recent anthologies such as *Cassilda's Song* (Chaosium) and *Mixed Up: Cocktail Recipes (and Flash Fiction) for the Discerning Drinker (and Reader)* (Skyhorse Publishing, Oct 2017). Her work has also been nominated for Best of the Net, the Hugo award, and two World Fantasy awards. Her debut collection, *Calls for Submission*, will be released May 2017 by Pelekinesis. You can find out more about her work and happenings at www.selenachambers.com, and *Nasty Writers* at www.nastywriters.com.

Farah Rose Smith is the founder and editor-in-chief of *Mantid Magazine*, a bi-annual arts and literary publication celebrating women writers and media creators from various backgrounds who illustrate the power of diversity through their identities and their work. The magazine is a platform for unusual, alternative, and underground fiction, and aims to serve as a platform for marginalized groups in the arts (LGBTQA+, women of color, and people with disabilities/the differently-abled).

She is also the founder/creative director of Grimoire Pictures, a small media company focusing on experimental filmmaking. Her work has received accolades at film festivals, including awards for Best Experimental Film (*The Atrocity Shoppe*) at the Shawna Shea Film Festival and Best Short Script (*Rapture*) at the Massachusetts Independent Film Festival. She is currently at work on her next film and first collection of short fiction, both due to be released in Autumn 2017. You can find out more about her work at www.farahrose92.wixsite.com and www.mantidmagazine.com.

SELENA CHAMBERS: As we are beginning this interview, it is Women In Horror month. While there are hundreds, if not thousands of us, working within this fine genre, there is still the presumption that women don't do horror, or science fiction, or any other speculative fiction genre. What it is assumed women write is chick lit, or feel-good historical fiction where someone marries rich and may be lucky enough to be widowed, or family/broken cis marriage novels—never anything about grit and guts, goblins and ghouls, intrigue or mayhem. So, since in the mainstream eye's anyway, we are anomalies, I have wondered: what is a nice girl like you doing in a genre like this?

FARAH ROSE SMITH: When it comes to the arts, the kind of strategic discomfort that women can weave, even when writing characters of other genders, is anchored in the social oppression that we face. The arts are that rare avenue where we can give ourselves permission to speak and to act. A society that views women as inferior and fragile fools and endangers itself. They want us all to be nice, don't they? Or, in the words of Gillian Flynn, the "cool girl." And we know that desire robs us of being entirely human in presence and in voice. So fuck the nice girl label. We're not nice girls. We're multi-faceted, fully capable and entirely human. Sometimes we're nice, sometimes we're furious. So many of us in the spec writing world want young writers of all genders to realize that it's OK to be furious, and important to challenge that fury in the way that suits them best. Don't be

NASTY WRITERS

A crossed-genre, literary magazine showcasing women writers with a particularly 'nasty' bent.

the nice girl. Be the nasty woman, and harness that energy to make a difference. Often times, that difference is made through art and writing.

I've always said that the horror genre is something of a dark labyrinth where women can return to experience some form of catharsis. I still believe that, but also have come to realize that it's also a place for us to exercise and exorcise our own innate brutality. Though women have made enormous strides historically (keeping in mind that these strides have unfortunately been skewed in favor of white women's rights, which hopefully will change in this renaissance of intersectionality), with the present resurgence of oppression impacting so many different kinds of people, it is so important for people of all genders to understand that speculative fiction is not only a place of sanctuary for women, but a place where they can thrive and subvert the kinds of things that keep them voiceless writing and in the world.

That's not to say that all writing has to be blatantly political or message-driven to have cultural weight. And it doesn't mean that we are required to be unkind or unapproachable. It means be a thinker, be objective, be self-sufficient, continue to educate yourself, practice self-care, and pursue a sense of healthy coexistence with others. I don't find genres where women are conventionally successful to be distasteful or lacking universally, though one does have to examine the impact that those works have.

In horror, women can be more honest about themselves and about others. We know there are no "nice girls." Men who choose to live with a glamorized idea about what a woman's role will suffer the consequences of putting that ideal on a pedestal. To be quite honest, the loss is theirs. At this point anyone who thinks women can't or don't do horror or speculative works simply have their head too far up their own ass and are caught up in the nostalgia of past generations. It's time to move on from casual misogyny.

And since it is Women in Horror Month, I will emphasize that it's critical that we prop up fellow women media creators by doing whatever one can to support them year-round, but especially this month when there are viable, recognizable platforms to do so. I cringe when women scoff at WiHM. When women oppose it, it reminds me that there are certainly tiers of oppression, even among those who proclaim to be inclusive, that need to be addressed before we can approach any sort of real sense of equality anywhere. Some have been blinded by their fortunes.

SC: Speaking of creating a welcoming space, I am really struck by your comment about how women can be more honest in horror. It really made me pause to think about why I write what I write. And you are right, the opportunity to discuss with abandon taboo subjects like our unique brand of body horror and psychological ghosts have much more potential than in say, realism. I was curious what aspects of your writing is more liberated by horror?

FRS: Horror allows me to purge all of the dark soul vomit up on a page where it can serve some other purpose rather than festering inside me. There are no real bells and whistles about it. I don't know that I could ever phrase it quite as eloquently as others. There aren't many places in literature or in life where a woman can be freely grotesque, freely depressive, freely sexual, without enormous push back. Horror has been my dark labyrinth and I allow myself to become lost in it as often as possible. When it comes to what I write personally, I find a sense of ease about being experimental, surrealistic, Avant-garde. These are the things that I want to write, and thankfully they materialize quite cozily in the realm of horror.

How about you, Selena? What aspects of your writing are more liberated by horror?

SC: Ha, I am liberated by horror probably to a fault. I talk about the fears of motherhood and pregnancy and how fucking awful cramps are. Sometimes, if I am in a particularly saucy mood, I'll describe my work to people as MensesPunk.

I grew up on Victorian literature, and everyone was either dying or miscarrying from pregnancy, and I always find it fascinating how Disneyfied childbirth is perceived now. So, horror allows me to explore the body in ways I have never felt comfortable doing in other avenues and genres.

FRS: And that's a big reason why women also gravitate towards writing by other women. Not because of some kind of trivial gender bias, but because there is a depth of understanding when it comes to the kinds of issues we face, both biologically and socially, that we want to believe someone else understands and can articulate.

This brings me to something else. Your story "The Last Session" included an intriguing mother-daughter dynamic. While portrayals of mothers and daughters aren't necessarily atypical in horror, I'm wondering if you feel, as I do, that there needs to be a greater variety of relationships between women portrayed in fiction? It's interesting that in horror, the only relationships we tend to see revolve around competition over men. Do you feel a sense of liberation writing about relationships between women that don't fall into that category?

SC: I do. I believe that we are basically the gradual accumulation of every relationship we've had—be it our parents, our friends, or our lovers. I am very interested in exploring how people can effect each other and help each other grow or wither. I would love to see more relationships between women that focus much less on male validation, or even sexual validation, and on how they shape each other psychologically. In writing about that, I feel I gain a further appreciation for the individual women in my life, and even more respect for their individual experiences.

FRS: I believe that as well. Which is why I have that deep appreciation for Silvina Ocampo. Something about the magic and horror of everyday ritual that so often stems from cumulative interpersonal experience. On the topic of appreciating women, sometimes it really does feel as though I have been stitched together by every woman I have ever crossed paths with in life, be it in person or through books. That feels like a real gift to reflect on amid all this modern national turmoil.

SC: You mentioned there needing to be a re-examination of the feminine, and I was curious where you were seeing that done (and by who) currently; and if not anywhere, what would you like to see writers doing to achieve this re-examination?

FRS: I have no doubt that there are stories out at present that are doing so precisely as I envision, or feel is necessary, though I haven't personally come across any modern material of the sort when it comes to expressive femininity. It may just be a niche interest of mine. Or as simple as my own laziness and entrenchment in previous centuries. There is no one way, and no RIGHT way, to be a woman, and womanhood of all kinds should be represented in fiction. Assigning lesser value to any mode of expression is damaging to individuals. So the tough girls, weak girls, smart girls, dumb girls, cool girls, nerdy girls, tomboy girls, girly girls, and all beyond and in-between, should

I am very interested in exploring how people can effect each other and help each other grow or wither. I would love to see more relationships between women that focus much less on male validation, or even sexual validation, and on how they shape each other psychologically.

have a place. In writing, as writers. Represented as fully human, as all gender identities, expressions, and orientations should be. As all races should be. As all abilities should be. The best writing allows us all to experience our own humanity and the humanity of others. I can certainly attest to the fact that women are writing about the challenges of womanhood, addressing both external/physical and internal/psychological aspects.

Gloria Steinem once said that "Women get more radical with age, men get more conservative." This brings to mind a key element of developing womanhood, which is the transitional tendency (often to a greater intensity) of feminist ideology over time. How do you plan to address/balance feminist evolution/ideological disparity and the often dissimilar perspectives of younger and older women in Nasty Writers?

SC: Isn't that an interesting observation? And I think it is really true. Of course, I can't really speak for the dudes, but I think the older you get as a woman, the less fucks you have to give, and so that makes you more amenable to what society views as radicalism in women—which is speaking up and out, mostly. But a lot of that also has to do with experience and environment. When you are in your teens, you don't have a lot of environmental diversity, and while it is probably different now with the presence of social media, I remember living a lot of my youth in a bubble. I fortunately had an intellectual mother who spent her pin money on books for me to read, but even then it was limited to what I could randomly find or hope to come across at the bookstore.

So, all of that is to say I had exposure to a lot of the intellectual foundations of feminism back then, but no a posteriori experiences that contextualized them until I reached college. But that doesn't mean there weren't issues within the high school experience that needed to be addressed. So, in the tradition of *Seventeen*, *Sassy*, and now *Teen Vogue* (who is just slaying it,), and that need for the feminist experience to be explored early on, *Nasty Writers* will feature a Young Adult section that will ideally feature work from teen writers, if they'll submit to me.

FRS: Are there particular women writers, activists, and/or figures, real or fictional, that potential contributors might look to that you feel embody the spirit and purpose of *Nasty Writers*?

SC: Oh, yes. You already mentioned Ocampo, she's certainly in the pantheon. A few others are: Pussy Riot. MANDEM, Kathleen Hannah. Audre Lord. Angela Davis, Andrea Dworkin. Rebecca Solnit. Mina Loy. Mary Wollstonecraft. Zora Neale Hurston. Victoria Woodhull. Hélène Cixous, Roxanne Gay. Porochista Khakpour, Jessa Crispin. Toni Morrison. Djuna Barnes. Shirley Jackson, Kathy Acker, Nella Larson, Nisi Shawl, Gloria Naylor, Ursula K. Le Guin, Angela Carter, Elsa von Freytag-Lorvinghoven, Octavia Bulter, Andi Zeisler, Maxine Hong Kingston, Simone de Beauvoir. Leonora Carrington, Gloria Steinem, bell hooks, Virginia Woolf, Camille Paglia, and my new poet girl crush Forugh Farrokhzad.

And while we're mentioning Leonora Carrington and Silvina Ocampo, with their work, and the other works of say, Mary Shelley and K. J. Bishop, women's writing has been critical to the development of Weird literature. What is it about Weird literature that lends itself to expressions of womanhood, and what do you hope to see less of and more of in the tradition as an editor and writer?

FRS: Historically, to be a woman in this world was to be oppressed, to be dehumanized, to be subject to the male gaze and agenda. For many around the world, this is still the case. Progress is a pendulum, and we are currently in the process of swinging so far back that we are threatening the ability of that pendulum to return to a place of "normalcy." But what is normalcy? Progress was never universal.

Every woman you mention may serve as a beacon for those women coming up through the roads that they paved for us. I'm particularly thrilled at your mention of Silvina Ocampo, as I believe that it should be the duty of every young lady writer to read *Leopoldina's Dream*. Not only because it is a valuable collection for various literary reasons, but because there is a tendency within the works to elevate the perspectives of young girls beyond what is typical for that kind of fiction. It is perhaps time for a re-examination of the feminine and how we may seek to spell out the strength and resolve in that mode of expression rather than perceived weakness of it.

And to speak of weakness! We must do so, and write weak women, because what strong woman has not been weak? I want to see stories about women who rise from near-insurmountable horror to become strong, not women who carry the toxic pseudo-masculine attributes that men want to assign based on their opinion of what strength is. I want to see stories from perspectives reaching around the world, illustrating fear, oppression, and resilience as we could not possibly recognize it from our perspectives. I want to see diverse representation as it pertains to sexual and gender identity, and strip away the entrenched shame that American people have around sex. I want to see female and non-binary villains who are as horrid as frightening as the males. We need better portrayals of characters with disabilities who aren't written through the able-bodied gaze and opinion of what constitutes their worth. I would be thrilled to read works that are able to balance the need for progressive, artful narratives while also subtly acknowledging the literary forefathers of the genre without pandering to them. The past was, the present is, and the future will be, but not without some cauldrons bubbling. But if water is to turn to steam, some bubbles will have to burst. We are beginning to see this type of thing manifest after the election, with a surge in activism, or at least the visibility of activism, as it pertains to women's issues.

The Women's March on DC in January and sister marches/demonstrations around the world made it clear that feminism, specifically intersectional feminism, is not only gaining ground, but has already become a movement to be reckoned with. What are your hopes for *Nasty Writers* when it comes to creating a platform for disparate identities and the experiences of diverse (LGBTQA+, POC, disabled/differently-abled) women?

SC: I have thought about this a lot because it's not like there aren't already well-established or even newer magazines and websites out there creating strong, intersectional identities and dialogues, i.e., *Bitch, Bust, ROAR, Dangerous Women*, etc. However, where *Nasty Writers* aims to be different, while in complete solidarity, from these publications is its emphasis on the importance of experimental and progressive creation rather than journalism and mainstream work to the womanhood resistance. I want the voices in *Nasty Writers* to speak to the more eternal aspects of resistance and womanhood, while exploring the very personal, first-hand experience of their own faced adversities, be it growing up Black, Middle Eastern, and/or Asian in the US, coping with mental health issues or with disabilities, or battling societal norms and mores with gender or body dysmorphia. Regardless of gender, each person is an individual with an individual battle, but through their experience, I believe there is a higher, Jungian story that readers can learn from, or at the very least, find a further empathy and understanding of how complex and nuanced womanhood (and you know, being human) is now and has been.

Which is why I love that *Mantid* is leveraging Weird fiction as a form of resistance. In your mission statement, you identify horror fiction as opening a door into the uncomfortable to discuss the taboo, the forbidden, the fearful. However, these stories, like any stories, have catered for too long to certain mainstream and elite expectations. Weird literature has always hovered on the periphery of this, sticking its toes in and out of all the various genre labels, focusing more on the ambiguous and mysterious unexplainable of being. However, I have yet seen anyone write of the Weird as political, which is what it seems like you are seeking to illustrate with *Mantid* What is it, in your mind, that Weird literature can bring to the political, and vice versa?

FRS: There is a story in *Cold Tales* by Virgilio Piñera called "The Dummy" that can be categorized as political-weird. An inventor becomes fixated on the President of his country and gains a private audience with him under false pretenses. It is a brilliant, exacting account of the ways in which brainwashing and manipulation spread like a virus and influence the masses, and is one of the greatest short stories I've ever read. Works like this are precisely the kind of thing that speak to past and present horrors on a national and global political scale, and how perception can lead to collective idiocy. Many of the stories in *Cold Tales* are a kick to the gut with political allegorical underpinnings.

> *Unfortunately, empathy cannot be taught, but those who possess it can harness it, congregate, and push for representation.*

Weird fiction can offer readers a chance to confront the abhorrent and unnerving psychologies interwoven in reality by making use of the fear that stems from the indefinable. The strange, inconceivable things that pave the road towards the kind of madness in fiction are also present in reality, though perhaps not in squamous or uncanny form.

Mantid is open to the kind of works that will examine these things, though I should note that the on-the-nose narratives are not always the most efficient way of confronting oppression. With great subtlety and care, even a story that on the surface seems to be apolitical can speak to modern circumstance in such a way that broadens the mind and empowers keen thinkers towards change. I would argue that they are better at doing that very thing, but this is my private perspective rather than something I would dictate to other writers. Ambiguous elements in the genre offer a place for us to insert our own thoughts, fears, and apprehensions, but many have been robbed of this by the cultural insistence that that which is undefined must, by default, cater to the white male perspective. Perhaps we need to examine the undefined as it surfaces in certain works and see interpretational allowances as a tool of inclusion, rather than a method of pandering to the elite as default. I do hope to see a shift in speculative fiction as it pertains to the elitism, as I think that we need to stop coddling the rich.

SC: That is what I find most inspiring and interesting in your mission statement—this renewed call for empathy. The need for art to expand and enrich based on the diversity of voices and experiences has always been literature's greatest achievement. However, as you and I know, the power of that empathy can only go as far as the voice can reach an audience. Is your call based on a dissatisfaction with genre and the voices it promotes, which is often touted and expected to be surface-driven, or is it more of a call against the publishing rat race, as a whole?

FRS: Unfortunately, empathy cannot be taught, but those who possess it can harness it, congregate, and push for representation. It can be done through writing, certainly, but it is probably best to avoid fixating on the outcome of one's work in that manner rather than just getting it out there somehow. Results may vary and no one can guarantee that something will be received as intended, especially by those so entrenched in the modern system, but what chance does anyone have if we all sit back and allow the status quo to continue? We all have different capacities for action, and certainly individual restrictions have to be taken into account, but there is always something someone can do to restore sanity. We must write. We must write. We must write.

For those who wish to contribute to *Mantid*, or anyone really, I would encourage making a point of reading works from authors who are from different backgrounds than your own. One of the richest elements of the weird fiction community is the absolute astonishing "mind-catalogues" of the writers, editors, and fans. People hand out recommendations like candy, and this is a magical thing! Nothing has brought me greater joy in the than seeing the enormous generosity of spirit that so many people have, which is a far cry from typical fandom snobbishness and exclusivity.

As for the publishing rat race as a whole, my concerns don't dwell heavily there, but only because I have an enormous respect for the power and influence of small presses. This stirs up a lot of heated conversations. Many writers simply aren't satisfied with that level of publishing and that's fine. Goals aren't universal. They should, however, be respected as places that allow innovative works to reach an audience. The good news is that many of these presses are run by progressive thinkers who are committed to publishing diverse voices.

I could, of course, delve into my personal experiences with misogyny and countless prejudicial "–isms", etc. in the theatre, film, and writings arenas, and how they spurred me forward to this present place, but these are things to be shared between friends and sisters. Sometime it's better to dwell on the present and what one can do to make the world a more hospitable place for the women and girls coming up after us. I am happy to take a hammer to the head for our daughters. It's incredibly hard to be the first to have an experience, or the first to step up and confront injustice, but if no one says or does anything, what chance will the women coming up after us have?

Speaking of firsts, that is precisely what the first issue of *Nasty Writers* is all about. We often look to other women as guides when trying to embolden ourselves and overcome the horrors of misogyny and patriarchal paradigms. Being at the helm of the magazine and a strong feminist yourself, do you have a "first" that stands out in making you the person that you are today? That may encourage women and especially young women to be open, to keep writing, and to contribute to the magazine? If not, is there a historic first that you feel particularly empowered by?

SC: I have always felt especially inspired by the life of Victoria Woodhull, who was the first woman in our country to run for president in 1872 (with Frederick Douglass as Vice President, btw). Woodhull was a spit-fire. She was born dirt poor in Ohio, and had no advantages other than will, determination, and spiritualism for a better life. She and her sister, Tennessee Claflin, utilized their clairvoyance to make money on Wall Street (first women to have a brokerage firm there), and Victoria was the first to speak on the Congressional floor. Her overall message to navigating a man's world—from voting to rape to business—was to just roll up in their space and inhabit it as an equal. And if they tried to shut you down, or out, you raised hell, you called wrongs out, and ultimately you beat them at their own game.

The Suffragettes and Abolitionists most remembered by history, Susan B. Anthony and Harriet Beecher Stowe especially, came from a more "gentle" background, and found Woodhull's tactics brazen, feral, and scandalous (especially when Woodhull publicly published against the hypocrisy of the famous reverend Henry Ward Beecher for his numerous affairs conducted while he denounced free-love from the pulpit). Anthony ultimately dismissed Woodhull from her Suffragette movement with rumor-mongering and defamation even though they utilized Victoria's tactics like just showing up to vote at the polls.

While I am no where near as radical (or loud) as Woodhull, or anyone really, I have always tried to adhere as much as possible to "shut the fuck up and do it or don't" principle of the Woodhull sisters. Because while the Suffragettes made great strides in their organization and vision, and get all the credit, history is full of women like Woodhull who had no time to sit around the parlor and think about shit. They had to get out

CALLS FOR SUBMISSION
SELENA CHAMBERS

there, throw elbows, get dirty with the boys, and get rowdy to make a name for themselves. I've had men try to intimidate me, gaslight me, yell at me, manipulate me and make me feel like I had no right to not only be in the same field/space as them, but even less right to share my voice or perspective. When that starts happening, I take a breath and think about how someone like Woodhull would handle it. And then I handle it.

So what does that have to do with writing? Two very important things, actually. Voice and determination. In publishing, both are critical and also vulnerable. You have to nurture and protect them, word by word, submission by submission, and not let intimidation kill them.

I like the idea of firsts for a magazine launch, only because a "first" for anything is the one moment where full potential and possibility emerge. Maybe the first of whatever won't be like the second or third, but it had to happen to put all other motions in action. I see this with *Mantid*'s first issue that featured diverse male writers as well as female writers. However, you have just revamped your guidelines and mission to make *Mantid* women and women-identifying only. What prompted this change? Was there a specific event, or a philosophical evolution, or just a space you weren't seeing that made you take the magazine toward this new mission?

FRS: The tone of the first issue was lighter, sassier, perhaps skewing more traditional horror than weird fiction. The second issue cut out excess content to focus on the fiction and poetry. It was at that point that I narrowed down the call to women and women-identifying writers only. I personally have no objections to men writing diverse characters, and try to encourage it as long as they approach it with an enormous sensitivity and commitment to research, but the bottom line is that when you have such wide guidelines for a magazine or anthology, you get an enormous amount of content. I was getting an absolute flood of submissions from men. People should be writing diversely, but that wasn't the only point here. The point was to honor diverse and oppressed women by giving them a platform. By narrowing it down, it allowed for a more thorough analysis of narrative content rather than a constant ringing in my head of "yikes, another dude!" Though I certainly have no excessive ideological objections regarding gender and publishing, I just thought it was time for the unsung to be given a chance.

The first issue of *Mantid* was a real ground floor operation. And by that I mean, I had never done anything like it before and had no clue what I was doing. With absolutely no reputation to build upon and very little knowledge of the publishing landscape, a small team of writers and artists brought together what turned out to be a starting point for something important. Sometimes it's worth it to start when you are clueless, if you have passion and a knack for organizing. In this way, you learn so much more than you could have ever envisioned learning. I encourage others to dive in head-first into whatever project, writing or otherwise, they wish to pursue. No one starts knowing everything (and no one ends that way either, no matter how hard they try to make you think they know it all).

It's in quiet spaces, soaked in youth and a sense of rebellion that innovation starts to take form.

In the documentary *The Punk Singer*, punk rocker Kathleen Hanna mentions women and girls being isolated in their bedrooms, and songwriting as a means of catharsis/empowerment. Hanna expressed her desire to bridge the gap between isolated women, bringing them together and out of seclusion. Riot Grrrls and Nasty Women have a lot in common. How will *Nasty Writers* bridge the gaps between women writers and help establish and embolden an empowered creative sisterhood?

SC: Yes, that description of how she wrote her *Julie Ruin* album spoke to me the most out of the whole documentary. In my mission statement, I write: "Please note, because we believe revolutions are cultivated in the bedrooms of teenage girls, we are especially interested in buying work from young adult women and women-identifying writers for our special, reoccurring feature 'Go to Your Room.'" That was 100% inspired by her reflections and comment on that experience.

I guess it spoke to me on several levels because it is definitely true that my intellectual awakening and cultural consciousness was bred in the petri dish of my room. In fact, I discovered Riot Grrrl, there, when I was 12 thanks to Seventeen magazine. I grew up in Florida, about as far removed from Olympia as you could be, and had a subscription to *Seventeen* and *Sassy* magazines. I didn't have access to zines yet, or even knew that they existed. All I had were mainstream rags aimed at girls, and then your typical rock mags like *Rolling Stone*, which was way different then than now, *CREEM*, etc. This was way before 2.0 whatever, so you basically just waited for things to find you, rather than you find them.

It was by Nina Malkin, published in the May 1993 issue. I remember seeing a picture of Kathleen Hannah half-naked and self-graffitied insults in sharpie over her body. And while the article was actually about infighting, the slogans, the vibe, and the just do it attitude of the movement was really inspiring to me. I'm not even sure how much I understood of the underlying politics just because it'd take a minute for me to get out in the world and experience it for myself. But yeah, I spent a lot of time reading, creating, and gestating in my bedroom, and it never occurred to me until I watched *The Punk Singer*, that anyone else was doing the same, or how sacred that space actually was at that time, and how hard it would be to recreate it in adulthood (what up, Virginia Woolf!).

And that is what I want *Nasty Writers* to do. I want it to take that idea of the internal experience and make it external. Right now, especially, there is the temptation to turn inward against the train-wreck that is becoming the current administration and give in to the fear and fatigue. I am hoping *Nasty Writers* will create a cerebral and metaphysical space for experimentation that can turn the fear and fatigue on its head and continue what women, both young and grown, have been doing since Enheduanna began writing and signing her poetry in the 23rd century BC.

FRS: Thinking back to your response about having an intellectual awakening in youth, something that was spurred by both zines aimed at girls (*Seventeen* was really important to me in those formative years as well) and punk rock, I'm brought to the reality we face as developing women acquiring knowledge. That, in a sense, it is still subversive to be a "thinking" woman. That in the process, we are criticized, demeaned, compared to each other, and ultimately even within the paradigm of "smart girl," become subject to patriarchal categorization. This, naturally, causes women with a desire to learn but without certain privileges or innate strength to fall by the wayside. So, on the challenges of being a thinking woman, navigating arenas dominated by men, I'm wondering how you personally, and how other young women may seek to, establish a sense of personal resolve and strength when it comes to educating themselves in culture, history, literature, etc.

> *Accept very early that you must educate yourself, alone, and come to your own conclusions. And once you've done that, seek the company of women who reflect your interests and aren't afraid to challenge your thoughts.*

SC: I have no idea how I've come to this conclusion, but for me art and literature is my religion. Writing, reading and learning is communing. In doing that, I have found my personal saints that speak to me, and so the first thing I'd advise is finding your Lady Patron Saint. For me, it was, and is Mina Loy, and once I fell in love with her and began reading and researching her life, she lead me to many other wonderful women that I admired and were inspired by.

Accept very early that you must educate yourself, alone, and come to your own conclusions. And once you've done that, seek the company of women who reflect your interests and aren't afraid to challenge your thoughts. They will be a great support group when you have to deal with disappointments within the larger realm. These two things will help you ascertain and solidify who you are. So, that, when you enter the larger realm, which will be dominated by men, or the mainstream that operates still by a very male-oriented ideal, they can't change you.

Oh, and one more thing—there is a lot to learn from the dead white guys, and there isn't anything wrong in studying them, but recognize their vision isn't yours, nor does it reflect your world, and what you take from them isn't theme or swagger, but style. Put them in your tool box, and use them to create your own themes and bravados.

Also important, is recognizing that behind every dead white guy is some other equally great writer who got lost in the footnotes…seek them out. They probably have more to offer in education than the idols. Some people get frustrated with the absolutes, like…you have to only read women or you are a betrayer to the Sisterhood.

It is very important to seek the women writers out, especially if they are reflecting your experiences. But, don't cheat your education by not learning what you can use from the canon against the canon, too. That is what has worked for me, anyway. What has worked for you, Farah?

FRS: I agree with the idea that art and literature can serve as a personal sanctuary. I approach it similarly, in that one creative or another will influence me, sometimes to the point of obsession, and the next step after consuming their contributions to the world will be looking into their contemporaries, their idols, etc. Perhaps oddly, my influences are more often painters than any other medium, though writers I hold in esteem (Hoffmann, Goethe, Schulz,), certainly put me on a specific literary interest "trajectory" of sorts. One that, I am sad to say, has been far too limited when it comes to learning about women.

Where I fail personally is that so many of my idols are the dead white guys, so it has become a personal mission to break that down and make a point to learn more about women who made contributions to culture. One particularly strong source of intrigue in my mind begin the women who functioned adjacent to great thinkers and artists…as there are tendencies in those dynamics that I find both fascinating and horrifying.

One of the hardest parts on this journey is when knowledge and community meet. I was, and continue to be, deeply intimidated by thinkers, writers, creatives of all kinds, but was fortunate enough to discover that when I jumped into what I thought would be an abyss of horror and comparison, that I found people, particularly women, who were both willing to share knowledge, and to challenge my own in healthy, productive ways. At the intersection of knowledge and inclusion, progress and innovation flourish.

SC: Well, I'm known as the Poe Girl, so I get it about having to step away from that paradigm. Luckily, Poe was a great advocate for women's writing, (and aped from them too, like Barrett Browning), so I did get to learn about some interesting women writers in conjunction with my early reading. But that is what I mean about searching for the footnotes.

Another example, for me, is Ernest Hemingway. I'm from Florida; Papa is in my environmental veins. But he doesn't write much from other than a man-motions perspective. But if you look into his life, he is surrounded by fascinating and brilliant women, some of whom may be even better at writing than him (i.e., Martha Gellhorn).

It's easier now, I think with the Internet, but I grew up having to seek things out…so it all was a lot of deduction and dumb luck.

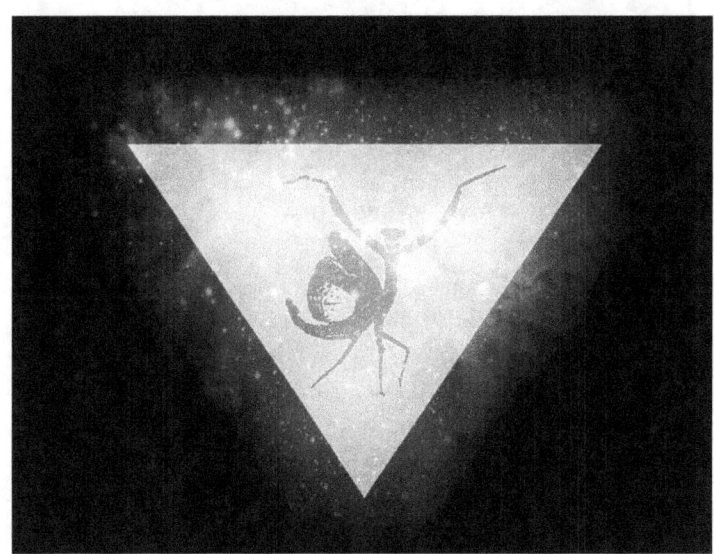

FRS: On the subject of Hemingway, I can draw a parallel between your observation and my observations when it comes to the artist Hans Bellmer. Unica Zürn was a pivotal part of his artistic career, but I can't say that I hear many speak of her other than as a subject in and accessory to his works, though I believe in France, her writing has drawn more attention over time. She wrote novels (*Dark Spring, The Man of Jasmine*) that were dark, surrealistic, and regretfully unsung in the Surrealist movement.

SC: Definitely. And same with Carrington (until recently), Lee Miller, and many of the Surrealist women.

FRS: The internet really is precious in these times, as reading seems to fall by the wayside. I think people get intimidated, perhaps, when they see the result of the journey of acquiring knowledge, but the journey and experience of reading, of learning, of consuming art and culture is really important, rather than what I think has become an over-emphasis on the artifacts of experience, though this is my strong personal bias coming into play. Coming from an art background and dabbling in everything from theatre to film to music, I often found that common strain… that there was a disconnect between journey and end result. I think it's important that we emphasis to women and young girls that the journey of learning, of experiencing, of creating is important.

I smile at the idea of young women approaching other women and forming bonds based in curiosity and sisterhood. I think this is an element that we sometimes don't examine as much as we need to. Unfortunately so many women in history succeed because they were approved of by men. I prefer to see women elevate each other.

SC: Me too. Although, I'd add that I think the groups of women have always been there, it is just they are lost even more to the shadows if they all weren't famous or notorious.

FRS: Absolutely.

SC: I totally agree that there is a disconnect between journey and end result. It is really normal online for people to present themselves as the expert—and because it isn't as sexy, there is very little regard given to process. Personally, I think the process is way sexier than achieving the actual expertise. But people want the glory that being an expert brings.

FRS: I guess I became a little jaded after experiencing the whole "I'm going to ask this new chick a bunch of questions and see if she's a REAL fan/reader/whatever." I'm sure you've experienced that as well. I used to try really hard to make it through those interrogations, but the older I get, the less fucks I give about what some snarky shit thinks about my presence or interests. Nowadays I find myself sitting quietly and being a sponge. It takes a lot of strength to be a sponge! And a good dose of social indifference. At the end of the day, learning and sharing knowledge matters. While there is a glamor to being the smarty pants, I've always sensed an inherent elitism mixed into the concept that is personally unappealing. Radical inclusion is a precious thing. Everybody should be able to learn. Everybody should be able to take the journey towards expertise.

SC: Oh, fuck yes. I have nothing to add other than preach it, sister! And the other thing I hate about that is everyone comes to their knowledge at their own pace…and so just because you don't know all the answers to Dudebro-Fanboys questions doesn't mean you won't be a real fan of the artist you are discussing later on. Unless Dudebro turns you off to the whole thing, which he often does sometimes.

FRS: That is a real problem. Because as much as I'd love to believe that all women have the strength, self-esteem, and resolve to continue in male-dominated fields, they don't. The meek tend to drop away. And that is a real problem, because sensitivity, fragility, heightened awareness… these are real ingredients to what makes an artist an artist, a thinker a thinker, etc. I have a soft spot for the so-called "weak" and "different" because I think there is a tendency to gloss over the contributions that certain kinds of people can make to society and culture.

SC: There is definitely a tendency in our current climate to speak over the meek or weak. We reward Extroverted behavior, and despite efforts of psychologists to reclaim Introversion, they still dominate. I mean, look at our fucking President. However, there is room for the internal ruminations, and that's why it is important for publications like *Mantid* and *Nasty Writers* (I hope) to exist—to give a welcoming space to those who may be intimidated to rumble with the loud and rowdy mainstream.

I have one last questions for you, and it regards your story "As Unbreakable As the World." You mentioned having a soft spot for the weak and silenced, and when I read your story, it felt like it was pertaining to a narrative about disability and possibly mental illness, something we don't have enough of (or that are well done enough, anyway, in genre). In discussing the need to examine narratives, what do you envision for that in regards to stories about disabilities?

FRS: That story was about the struggle to reconcile one's identity and worth in an ableist world. Weakness and strength are assigned value and definition based on arbitrary, human-centric things. Perceived worth stemming solely from achievement marginalizes people with physical and mental differences. It is far too rigid a method for determining what kind of contributions an individual may make to society, and whether or not those contributions deem someone "worthy" or equal to the rest. In that story, the idea is explored that a marginalized individual is not at home in a society that deems them either beneath the standard of normalcy or exceptional based on low expectations. That such perceptions are maddening and isolating. These individuals are (to themselves) quite normal and find the problem exists in navigating the world that they are forced to live in.

Most narratives that incorporate people with physical and mental differences are ableist in that they objectify individuals with disabilities for the benefit of able-bodied people. This furthers the "inspiration porn" agenda in which people disabilities are used as feel-good tools rather than regarded as fully human. I would encourage people to look up the TED talk by the late Stella Young, called *I'm Not Your Inspiration*. In it she emphasized the fact that we are more disabled by our society than by our bodies and minds, and that disability needs to be seen as normal, not exceptional. Representation in the arts should be steered towards portraying the reality of individual experience rather than falling back on persecutory falsehoods and objectification. On the topic of mental illness, it needs to be dealt with as true illness, and once again, this requires sensitivity and thorough research.

Naturally when I think of the politics of different-ability in these times, my mind rushes to The New York Times reporter Serge Kovaleski. What I find demoralizing is the fact that, here we have an individual who has existed and achieved in the world as legitimately as any other, who has now not only had to face the perils of navigating the ableist-constructed world (and has done a badass job doing so, by the way), who had to experience that disgusting mockery and the media fallout that reduced him to his condition. The whole ordeal was infuriating on so many levels, and I could drive myself mad thinking about the various philosophical nuances one may try to employ to deal with the problem of the leader of the free world being a cavalier ableist. The sad reality is this: the shock of able-bodied people was far stronger than our shock. That moment captured the experience of what we face in life every day. Ableism is business-as-usual. So is it that surprising that we would want better representation in the world of art and literature? The places of sanctuary afforded to everyone else? Or at least representation that is honest and realistic? I think being treated as fully human is long overdue, in art and in life.

SC: A-femme. ∎

GREAT AMERICA

(OR A WALL OF WORDS WITH PICTURES)

POP? MY BUDDY GARY IS SAYIN' SOME AWFUL BAD THINGS ABOUT AMERICA.

HE SAYS AMERICA WAS NEVER GREAT BECAUSE RELIGIOUS, ETHNIC, RACIAL, AND SEXUAL-ORIENTATION GROUPS HAVE ALWAYS BEEN OPENLY DISCRIMINATED AGAINST.

WOMEN WERE MUCH LESS PRESENT IN POLITICS AND THE PROFESSIONAL WORLD. EDUCATIONAL INSTITUTIONS HAD POLICIES EXCLUDING OR RESTRICTING ENROLLMENTS BY MINORITIES. EVEN THE US MILITARY HAD LAWS CRIMINALIZING NON-HETEROSEXUAL BEHAVIORS.

WAS AMERICA EVER GREAT?

OF COURSE AMERICA WAS GREAT, JOHNNY! I'LL TELL YOU ALL ABOUT IT!

WHEN THE TROOPS CAME HOME FROM WORLD WAR 2 WE FOUND THAT WE COULD MANUFACTURE ALL KINDS OF JUNK AND SELL IT TO THE WORLD. WE'D DECIMATED OUR INDUSTRIAL COMPETITORS: MOST OF EUROPE AND JAPAN WERE DEVASTATED. FACTORIES AND WORKERS WERE BOMBED OUT.

IT WAS PRETTY EASY TO GET A GOOD PAYING JOB EVEN WITH NO COLLEGE EDUCATION: THE GREAT AMERICAN FORTUNES OF THE PRE-COMPUTER AGE WERE MADE BY THE CARNEGIES, FORDS, AND ROCKEFELLERS WHO EMPLOYED THOUSANDS OF LABORERS TO BUILD THINGS.

GOLLY! WHAT'S A COMPU-

DON'T INTERRUPT, BILLY.

BY CHRISTIAN GOODRICH

COLLEGE TUITION WAS CHEAP BECAUSE IT WAS LESS IMPORTANT TO GET A JOB. YOU GRADUATED FROM HIGH SCHOOL, GOT A JOB NEARBY IN A FACTORY, AND IMMEDIATELY AFFORDED BUYING A HOUSE, A CAR, AND A WIFE. THE AMERICAN DREAM.

BUT THE SUPERPOWERS REBUILT AND DEVELOPING COUNTRIES INDUSTRIALIZED THEMSELVES IN THE FOLLOWING DECADES CREATING GLOBAL COMPETITION. MANY OF OUR FACTORIES, UNABLE TO COMPETE, CLOSED. OWNING A HOME AND SUPPORTING A FAMILY BECAME HARDER FOR THOSE WHO WEREN'T COLLEGE GRADUATES IN THE RIGHT FIELD.

NOW ONLY POORER COUNTRIES TRY TO BUILD THEIR ECONOMIES PRIMARILY ON A BLUE-COLLAR FACTORY BASE. ALL THE ADVANCED COUNTRIES IN THE WORLD ARE SHIFTING FROM MANUFACTURING TO COMPUTER AND KNOWLEDGE-BASED ECONOMIES.

I dunno why illustrations of those are necessary...

YOU SAID THAT COMPUTER WORD AGAIN. IT'S STRAINING THE 1950'S MILIEU...

DO YOU WANT A SMACK, JIMMY?

TLDR: GLOBALIZATION HAPPENED. THE JOBS AREN'T COMING BACK.

WOMEN'S MARCH ON WASHINGTON AND ASSOCIATED SISTER MARCHES

On Saturday, January 21, a massive movement took to the streets. The Women's March on Washington and related Sister Marches all across the USA and throughout the entire world drew between 2.5 million and 6 million people out in often lousy weather to protest against not only the profoundly anti-woman policies of the incoming Trump administration but, in the words of the Sacramento Women's March, "[t]he rhetoric of the past election cycle [that] has insulted, demonized, and threatened many of us. Immigrants of all statuses, Muslims and those of diverse religious faiths, people who identify as LGBTQIA, Native people, Black and Brown people, people with disabilities, survivors of both domestic violence & sexual assault—and our communities are hurting and scared. We are confronted with the question of how to move forward in the face of national and international concern and fear."

The turnout was staggering and is considered to be the largest protest event in American history. Following are photos from marches in Sacramento, Tallahassee, and Washington, DC.

Washington, DC photos courtesy of Eric Schaller

Washington, DC photos courtesy of Eric Schaller

Sacramento photos courtesy of Rachael Cowan and Glenda Goyne

Writer Selena Chambers, pictured left with the "Tiny Hands/Big Business" sign, reports that over 15,000 participants showed up from all over Florida to march from Tallahassee's Railroad Square arts district up to FAMU campus, the historical black college. At FAMU, people who wanted to listen to Planned Parenthood representatives speak could at the recreation center, or turn around and march to the Capitol (where people were being deterred to do so because of a lack of permit). Chambers, alongside friend-sisters Lisa Bullington and Sheri Nilles-Marshall trudged through the pouring rain to join thousands others in chanting, solidarity, and taking to the streets.

ATLANTA: FOUR MARCHES, THIRTEEN DAYS

[Anya Martin]

MLK DAY MARCH AND RALLY, MONDAY JANUARY 16

The MLK Day March in Atlanta is a long tradition, but then Atlanta is Dr. King's hometown. Fourth time for me marching and the second time not with a political campaign, General Wesley Clark in 2004 and Barack Obama in 2008. Met up with Ray Dafrico at a Starbucks downtown. Ray's a friend from back in the Scene (founding member of almost-legendary punk band The Nightporters). Ray and I knocked on doors together for the Hillary Clinton campaign in November and he went on to launch the Atlanta-based Donald Trump Resistance Society (DTRS). Leading the march are the unions with big banners and bullhorns. Easy to join them chanting and singing the workers' songs that my dad played on the record player when I was little. "We shall not be moved." A father, who I later learn is a local activist lawyer, and his two small daughters walk behind us with their signs, one daughter on his shoulders. Welcome, love and community fill the air.

Our friend Nancy Larson joins us. About halfway down Sweet Auburn Avenue, transitioning from traditional white downtown to what was once called the "richest Negro street in the World," we leave the Unions to watch for a while—environmental groups, LBGT rights, disabled, church groups, African-American community groups, marching bands and QuikTrip employees. All skin colors, faces smiling. People treat Ray like a rock star for his "Dump Trump" sign and ask to pose with him holding it.

As the march ends, speeches and music. A meditative moment at the King Memorial to pay our respects at the tomb of Dr. King and Coretta Scott in the center of the long reflecting pond. Children pause, too, transfixed and quiet. On the walk back to Ray's car, we take our group photo under the giant mural of John Lewis, who walked with Dr. King and represents Georgia's fifth district, most of Atlanta's city limit. I don't realize it until later but today was the calm before the storm. Barack Obama was still president. Hope still held that some unknown miracle could prevent Trump's ascendancy. Perhaps the spirit of Dr. King was sending us strength for the fight ahead.

Photo courtesy of Anya Martin

ATLANTA MARCH FOR SOCIAL JUSTICE & WOMEN, SATURDAY JANUARY 21

Torrential rain and high winds, thankful for the long, hooded transparent plastic raincoat my mom bought in Finland probably in the 70s and my paisley rubber cowboy boots. I drive first to a quilting/knitting shop near me. I didn't intend to wear a pink pussy cat, but a friend knitted one for me and left it there for pick up. The ladies there hand me three tote umbrellas to give away. The parking lot at the MARTA (transit) station almost full but I find a space. Lots of mothers and groups of little girls. I give away the umbrellas immediately and am thankful I have credit on my MARTA card and don't have to stand in the mob buying train-fare. Crowded platform, train standing-room only. Once downtown, I get off a stop earlier than most to meet Ray at the Dunkin Doughnuts. The wind feels like it's going to blow me over as I walk the three blocks in sheets of hard rain. We wait for Ray's daughter and her boyfriend, and receive texts from people at the march start that it's been delayed by an hour due to the rain. Someone else texts she's still at a MARTA station in the suburbs and it's packed with people trying to buy fare and cram onto the train. Rain or no rain, that's Atlanta—late to everything, including a protest. But they are coming despite the rain, the wind, the pain in the ass of parking and waiting for public transit.

Finally, Ray's daughter arrives and since I didn't manage to make my own sign (which would have been soaking wet and destroyed probably anyway), Ray asks me to choose and I get the rock-star "Dump Trump" sign. Maybe I could have been more clever—but I'm in the mood to get right to the point. The rain slows to a drizzle, then finally stops while we are walking. This March is meant to happen. More and more people converge as we skirt the edge of Centennial Olympic Park and head down to the far end to the Center for Civil and Human Rights, built to house Dr. King's personal papers. The crowd already impressive for its size, unlike any I have seen downtown since the 1996 Olympics—*before* the bomb. You have to understand—Atlantans don't come downtown unless it's for work or there's a game, a concert, a charity walk or DragonCon.

Our Millennial companions abandon us. Ray and I proceed towards a rumored rally with speeches on the other side of the CCHR. We scale a fence and maneuver a muddy slope. I don't slide nor fall despite the slick—rubber boots caked with moist Georgia red clay. The crowd too thick to make it further. We line up on the side street and wait. Volunteers tell us to clear

Photos courtesy of Anya Martin

33

a path because Representative John Lewis and others will be passing this way to lead the march. Cheers from the crowd as the man of the hour who just stood up to Trump approaches. "Fighting Fifth!" These Atlantans are still angry about Trump's tweets that the city is "horrible," "falling apart" and "crime-infested" after Lewis called him out, so Lewis is even more of a hero than ever! I snap a pic of him shaking a woman's hand with a BLACK LIVES MATTER sign raised high behind him that ends up getting shared a lot on Facebook.

Wait, wait, wait. More march leaders pass by on the other side including local celebrity and LBGT rights activist Baton Bob, and later I learn from photos, members of the Fugees family, a soccer team and school for refugees founded by my Smith College sister Luma Mufleh. Between John Lewis, Baton Bob and the Fugees Family, the Atlanta march doesn't face some of the criticism about inclusiveness that other Womens Marches around the nation do. We can't see any movement but hear the march has started and people who got there after us are just stepping straight into it, my friend Liz who just got there off MARTA confirms.

When we finally move, everything accelerates. Ray on his bullhorn: "Show Me What Democracy Looks Like!" Crowd: "This Is What Democracy Looks Like." Time begins to blur. I note the diversity around me—hijabs, LBGT, mothers and daughters but also fathers and sons. Palpable energy driven by anger and hope that surely all of us can make a difference because we simply showed up one day after Trump's inauguration. Liz joins us about 10 blocks down, and I realize suddenly that I have seen NO COPS. I mean NO COPS. Cop cars and officers stood at every street corner on the MLK March. Are they not worried about this crowd? Should we be a little insulted that we're not considered a threat? As we turn up past CNN Center, cops finally. But very relaxed cops. We cross over the long bridge curving around the downtown skyline and down a hill. At its foot, the cops and protestors are high-fiving and smiling. I snap and post a pic. The Atlanta PD post their own pics and videos of this.

About two hours after we began at the CCHR, we head uphill to the Georgia State Capitol with its gold dome. Protestors lean and sit on its walls but behind the metal fence a handful of big white good old boy state troopers glare at us with derision. Someone points at snipers on the roof. We pour out onto the street in front of the Capitol, and some people peel off towards MARTA. It takes a while to figure out how to get into the fenced area where the speeches are and we miss most of them (John Lewis again and other state leaders such as Georgia House Rep Stacy Abrams who is rumored to be planning a gubernatorial run next year), but arrive just in time

Photo courtesy of Anya Martin

to see the Fugees Family. A group holds up big letters: I-L-L-E-G-I-T-I-M-A-T-E. A guy with long dark hair and a stunning gold mask in a black leather jacket has a sign that sums it all up: HONESTLY THERE ARE TOO MANY PROBLEMS WITH THIS ADMINISTRATION TO SUMMARIZE IN ONE SIGN. The final count for protestors is estimated at over 60,000. Some complain that Atlanta should have done better, but given the crazy hostile weather and our city's recent complacency despite its Civil Rights legacy, I feel like we did really well.

#NODAPL & SCIENCE MARCH, SUNDAY JANUARY 29

Maybe 400 gather in Piedmont Park between 11 a.m. and noon. Sun shining, chilly so I wear a knit hat—but choose one made by another friend in many colors. I'm here to Stand with Standing Rock for #NODAPL, terrified that the protest led by Native Americans in North Dakota will end with terrible violence when the Trump administration allows law enforcement to dismantle the camps and forcibly remove everyone. I have two signs on thick black boards I found in my garage, rescued from a neighbor's trash. I discovered they work perfectly with colored chalk and write double-sided NATIVE LIVES MATTER & BLACK LIVES MATTER and WATER IS LIFE & NO DAPL. Again I meet up with Ray. The organizer is late so another organizer from a group that is trying to unify all Atlanta protests takes over. After a short rally, we start up 14th Street towards Peachtree Street, cops following us and telling us to stay on the sidewalk. Again we chant loudly and march fast. I let a woman who doesn't have a sign hold my WATER IS LIFE/NO DAPL. As we reach Peachtree, which is busy, horns honk in solidarity. You can tell the opposition because they keep their windows up and glare at us like we're some caustic irritant—flies or mosquitoes. We end at Bank of America, one of the banks that invested in DAPL and other pipelines, then the group winds toward MARTA. Overcast now and wind picks up. Ray and I take a lunch break at a nearby soup and salad place. We sit at the counter by the

window and I put my signs in the window so passers-by can see them. After we eat, I take out poster board and markers which Ray had stashed in his car, and make my sign for the next protest (MUSLIM LIVES MATTER #nobannowall) which starts at 4 p.m. at the Hartsfield-Jackson International Airport. The African-American restaurant staff tell us how supportive they are and how they wish they didn't have to be working and could go to the airport with us. A probable Republican family at the table next to me occasionally glances over and says nothing.

RALLY FOR REFUGEES, ATLANTA AIRPORT, SUNDAY JANUARY 29 4–7 P.M.

Ray and I disembark MARTA with a crowd of other people with signs, airport security officers directing us to go immediately outside. Across the South Terminal (Delta) baggage claim pick-up area, a crowd has already gathered even though it's not yet the official start time of 4 p.m.—hundreds, maybe a thousand. We work our way towards our friends Nancy and Michael. I end up leaning on the front railing where the cars stream by to

drop off and pick up passengers. Protestors keep coming and coming and coming. More and more and more. At first they cross the street to join us, then security gives up directing them to do so and they start to fan out and take up the entire length of baggage claim, holding their signs, shouting. Again some cars and SUVs keep their windows up and look irritable, but many more honk, their occupants yelling their support, raising their fists, taking pics and video with their phones. They've never seen anything like this. I've never seen anything like this, not just at the airport but anywhere.

Word passes through the crowd that John Lewis is here, and he passes through the heart of the throng near me, shaking hands, tailed by Atlanta Mayor Kasim Reed who, I suppose, thought he was here to win hearts and minds, and instead was greeted by loud chants of "Make Atlanta A Sanctuary City." The vehicles continue to stream by. A food truck advertising falafel and gyro wraps driven by the man with the sign that he is a proud Iranian immigrant! A young woman in the pink hijab standing in the sunroof of a black SUV with a smartphone taking pics of us and shaking her fist in solidarity (my favorite photo—it's hard to chronicle when you're holding a sign and chanting and I never get a photo of the Iranian foodtruck owner even though he circles several times). Carloads of Islamic immigrants, some in hijabs, some holding signs in the windows. Joy. Not terrorists. Happy to be in America, and they don't judge us, just Trump and our leadership.

The crowd finally thins out on our side after two hours, and Ray, Nancy and I cross over to the front of the terminal where protestors linger around a man waving a large Syrian green, orange and white flag and another with a bullhorn, leading the crowd in chants and songs. Beauty and love radiate. I speak to a young woman from Iran who came here to study. Then someone comes out the airport sliding doors and yells that the police are harassing and threatening to cuff and arrest any protestors who come inside and how they need to come inside. The Syrian men heed the call and enter, trailed by many of those who remain.

We follow, not sure what we are getting ourselves into. A guard directs us towards MARTA and the vibe is we've had our time, and now they want us to leave. We don't see what happened, but we don't hear of any arrests in the news.

Before we board the escalator to the tracks, a MARTA security guard thanks the protestors for coming. On the train, I'm left with the thought that people who have every reason now to hate America showed so much love today. Four protests, and with each the momentum builds. This is the new way of life in America. Make a sign, take a walk, shout loudly, make ourselves heard. ■

Photos courtesy of Anya Martin

POETRY

THE SIN THAT STAINS THE SOUL

[Jason A. Zwiker]

you saw him there but something
deep inside said
no, I didn't
and every day, between three and four, it rained
you heard him tap his heels in time

as he sang his little ditty
one day, you'll finally see me
standing where I've always stood
I own this world already

what you've forgotten fills a teacup
an ocean, what you've never known
this is the sin that stains the soul

one day, the Reverend poured his coffee
inside the Circle K, watched bubbles
spin and break upon its skin
and the sun that split and smeared itself
across the brutal sky was no sun of man
his smile was like a book of revelation
as you heard the Reverend say

I need bones to sink in my new found church
he sipped, said *God, that's good*

this world is long overdue, by God, again
for a reminder of what it means
to be truly wronged by a professional

what you've forgotten fills a teacup
an ocean, what you've never known
this is the sin that stains the soul

you saw three, then four, suns at work
returning waters to the sky
you saw the holy man and his shadows
and you could have sworn you heard
one day, you'll finally see me
standing where I've always stood
I own this world already

and the part of you that saw him knew
it was safer, for now, to think
no, I didn't
I didn't see
what I just saw
even as he tapped his heels and split the sky

and every day, between three and four, it rained

38

OUR CENTURY'S SONG

[S. L. Edwards]

And though your voice may wear
Through screaming, your lungs may tear
Though your feet might tear, tire and ache
Though your heart, time and time again, will break
I beg you, dear child, please go on
Never stop singing your century's song.

Your struggle is being, an unfortunate meaning
And they will always tell you that you must dreaming.
Bend your ear, but do not give in to fear
Your fight will continue into next year,
And perhaps even after that.
But it will not be the last.

Make your struggle your armor and shield
And your pain a powerful sword to yield.
The world might be vicious and it might be cold
But it will be better when you are old.
And you might hand it to younger hands still
And with it, they will do what they will.

THE DONALD EPIGRAM

[S. L. Edwards]

In Memory of Osip Mandlestam

Our movement no longer feels free or certain
Our words blocked by a hateful curtain.
But whenever there is fear in the air,
It stems from the New Yorker with matted hair,
The tiny ten-things that he calls fingers,
A face where an orange smear lingers,
Thin lips and thinner eyes,
The glimmer of ignorance and lies.
Surrounded by men who nod and smile,
Collecting their dignity and consuming their bile,
Some nod and some move for power.
With pen strokes, and they have taken the hour.
He throws insults like darts
One for the body, another for the heart.
He rolls off hatred like a good taste on his tongue.
He wishes to breath it in, to take it into his lungs.

THE WENDIGO SICKNESS

[Jason A. Zwiker]

if I ask you
to fill your begging bowls with the western skies
and bring them to the scales
to measure them

against the weight of the eastern skies
against the weight of the northern skies
against the weight of the southern skies

and you tell me it can't be done
how can you claim to love me?

one day

we wandered the streets of a faraway city
counting the people as we passed them
our error increased with every scratch
on the chalkboards of our minds
our thoughts were unclean
because we were empty

there was nothing inside

there will come another day
a day when I'll ask you

did you sleep, my angel
debauched and deadened
to the world around you

or did you toss and turn
snatching ragged scraps
of dream from the silence in-between

I'll say this

my heart is through with me
it's done, wants out
I wake to it slamming itself
against the bones of its cage as my brain
lights up like a flash of thermite in the night

do you understand? have you
known this place before or am I describing
a city to the blind

they left us alone in the heart
of those dark woods in winter
what would you have had me do?

I've no desire
to add to your suffering
only to ask you this

do you believe that hungry ghosts
speak of being hungry ghosts
and welcome their newborn heirs
by stirring their appetites
while pinching shut their mouths and throats

or do they say
this is what it takes
to be a man in this world

I will feed you
and I will teach you
to feed yourself
and every bite you swallow
will create the need for two bites
and every two bites, the need for ten
and every ten, the need for a thousand
and you will never feel at ease

all you'll know is a hunger so sick that the sight
of anyone other than yourself
at table will make you shake with rage

what makes you so certain you're not in Hell already?

there are things about this world
I'd rather not know
this suppuration of the thin
skin we call civilization
can't go on forever

do you remember the last time we dreamed
we dreamed it was dripping
red
gravy, God
do you remember
a time before we were buried
in this billowing white, a time before
the walls closed in
don't

those are happiest who forget
the meat is sweetest at the bone

SEVEN POEMS BY DELMIRA AGUSTINI

[translated by Scott Nicolay]

SNAKE WOMAN

In my dreams of love, I am a snake!
Gliding and rippling like a current;
Two pills of insomnia and hypnotism
For my eyes; the tip of an enchantment
Forms my tongue…and I lure prey sure as tears!
I am the abyss distilled.

My body is a ribbon of delight,
It glides and ripples like a caress…

And in my dreams of hatred, *I am a snake!*
My tongue is a venomous fount;
My head a luciferous diadem,
Of death, in a deadly sidelong line
My pupils lie; and my bejeweled body
Is the thunderbolt's sheath!

If I dream so of my flesh, so is my mind:
A long body, long as a snake,
Vibrating eternally, *voluptuously*!

THE VAMPIRE

In the lap of the sad afternoon
I invoked your sorrow…To feel that it
Was to feel your heart! How pale you grew
Even your voice, your eyelids like wax,

They lowered…and you fell silent…You looked
As if you heard Death pass by…I who opened
Your wound bit into it--did you feel me?
It was like biting into a honeycomb's gold!

And I squeezed harder, a traitor, sweetly
Your heart wounded mortally,
By the rare and exquisite dagger
Of a nameless evil, until I'd bled it dry with cries!
And the thousand mouths of my damned thirst
Held open to that fount your breaking opened.

Why was I the vampire of your bitterness?
Am I the flower of some dark species' line
Who feeds on sores and drinks in tears?

FROM EL ROSARIO DEL EROS (THE ROSARY OF EROS): FIVE POEMS

BEADS OF MARBLE

I, the marble statue with its head on fire,
Cooling my temples with cold and white I pray…
Entwine in one gesture with palm or star
Thy body, that hypnotic alabaster prize
Carved by pure kisses and polished by the ages;
Serene, as if armored in moonlight;
Whiter than if thou wert the foam of our Race,
And from the tabernacle of thy chastity,
Lift to me the secret lotus of thy soul;
Let my shadow kiss thy mantle of stillness,
Which growing, growing, will wind me up in Thee;
Then my flesh will be lost in thine…
Then my soul will be dissolved in thine…
Then it will be glorious…and we will be a god!

—Love of whiteness and cold,
Love of statues, lilies, stars, gods…
Give them to me, my God!

BEADS OF SHADOW

Black beds produce the most potent
Rose of love; they out down roots in death.
Grand beds spread with sadness,
Carved with a dagger and canopied
With insomnia; the open
Curtains speak of dead braids;
As good as extra heads
On lush pillows like sisters:
Plinths of Dream and steps of Mystery.

So if on a bed like death's own flower,
We drop weeping, like fervid fruit
Grown ripe in passion, in spirits and flesh,
They will be of beautiful forsaken kinds,
Kissing the profile of the stars
Treading the tresses of the palms!

—Glory to the dark love,
Like Death it rots and exalts
Give it to me, my God!

BEADS OF FIRE

Lock the door at the first hint of caress,
Roughly strip the lily bare...
"Silk is a sin, nudity is divine;
And a yielding body is a divan of delight."

Spreading arms...let every being have wings,
Or a warm lyre sweetly exhausted
Of silence and of song...later, in the cold
Beyond of a mirror like an inclined lake,
See the beast whose Olympic labor brings forth life...

Red love, my love;
Blood of worlds and blush of heavens...
Give it to me, my God!

BEADS OF LIGHT

Far off as in death
I feel the flames of a life turning ever toward me,
Slow fire formed from sleepless eyes, stronger than
If it gilded all my here from unfathomable there.
Over land and seas its horizon is my scowl,
Like a restless swan asleep on my dream
And its muffled step of absence and reproach
Gentle patter of ownerless dogs
That have already gnawed hunger, sadness, and night
As they drag their chains of mystery and reverie.

Love of light, a river
That is the crystal path of Good.
Give it to me, my God!

FALSE BEADS

The black crows are starving for rosy flesh;
In deceitful moonlight I reflect my sculpture,
They shatter their beaks, hammering the mirror,
And as I escape in irony, untouched and glorious,
The black crows fly off full of rosy flesh.

Cold derisive love
Marble that ennui varnished with fire
Or lily robed in rose by a blush,
Let me have it always, my God...

O fertile rosary,
Living necklace encircling
The throat of the world.

Chain of Earth
Fallen constellation.

O magnetic rosary of snakes,
Glide to an end between my knowing fingers,
That in the smile of your fifty teeth
My life lit up with one great kiss:
A rose of lips.

Delmira Agustini was born in Montevideo, Uruguay, in 1886 to a family of Italian immigrants. She began to write poetry when she was 10 years old.

She formed part of the Generation of 1900, along with Julio Herrera y Reissig, Leopoldo Lugones and Rubén Darío, whom she considered her teacher.

Agustini specialized in the topic of female sexuality during a time when the literary world was dominated by men. Her writing style is best classified in the first phase of modernism, with themes based on fantasy and exotic subjects.

She married Enrique Job Reyes in August 1913 and left him a month later. Their divorce was finalized in June 1914. A month after that, Reyes fatally shot Agustini twice in the head and afterwards committed suicide. She was 27.

FIGHT BACK

OUR INSOLVENCY

[Jeremy Hoevenaar]

Now it's morbs
with a side of the
haptic willies. Up-
wards of medium loose
cannon, my replacement
head's a fledgeling life-
hack hunched in dazzle
camouflage and lightly
double billed as a rest-
orative wringing in
of Twenty-Seventeen,
a proper name for a com-
promised kick in the teeth
(those bad teeth over there),
swank reissues of scum
and villainy outdoing
an opt-out's stature
to sweep our will
to acceptance. Off
to launch a habit-
able spore for fan poetry's
built sake b/w option to
choke up or out. Fully
feeling this new enteric
narrative, display's misty
for a two bit 8-bit poli-
tics of convenience,
bluntly asymmetrical
war-hair sworn in with
venal abruptitude,
popping gestalt wheelies
in a world where no
worm's left unturned

OUR INSOLVENCY

[Jeremy Hoevenaar]

Me, I'm genuinely
going to where going
actually meets truly
interested. Everything
works that works,
a version in the lurch
of a menu loop, pause
or no pause. Morning light
continues its slack con-
figuration or tip-off lined
with millennial innuendo,
newsy and proceeding
snackishly, punctum-packed
with nutrient-dense wiggle-
room. Unborn to hover,
parody's on the pre-
existing prowl and
quivering to draw a serious
click. You will down-
cycle, a lot, instantiating
for a laugh. Internalized
language wrinkles with
the year's grain, void not
for rescale, standard
inversions still irksomely
buoyant, slashed or dashed
as needed to coast on
these columnar strides
of wrongful compression.
You throw me the idol,
I'll show you the life of the mind

THE PARABLE OF THE MERCIFUL MOTHER DUCKS

[Christopher Ropes]

In mercy, we mother ducks wander,
Counting our ducklings until we find
That one has gone missing.
By compassion we are torn, and we
Pluck our breasts bare and bloody.

In mercy, we feel entirely alone.

In mercy, we watch the young black men
Die and die and die, and we wonder why
They don't give the uniforms to us,
We who count our ducklings and search
For any who have wandered astray.

In mercy, we protest the wars and rapes
And make our voices loud, growing more shrill
With every kill and every lost soul
Dead drunk or just dead, flopped on
Merciless pavement in front of the Greyhound
Station.

In mercy, we wonder if our shrill voices

Demanding justice are just saying, "Quack.
Quack quack quack." Are we not heard
Or not understood or do they hear
Perfectly well and understand perfectly well,
But they are the predators whose bellies
Are filled by all the world's missing ducklings?

In mercy, we slide beneath the waters,
Intending to never surface again.

In mercy and in confusion, we curl in on ourselves,
We crawl back into an egg and change.

When we hatch again, we have grown
Fangs and claws and soft feathers are replaced
By spines and bristles.
In fury, our shrill quacks have become
A need to riot.

THE APOCALYPSE KID AND THE OLD MAN

[Christopher Ropes]

Outside my window in choking
Early AM grayness and far away,
I hear the clang, the bang of
A dumpster lid, slammed over and over
By some kid looking for that free lunch
He was promised, that American Dream,
Pawing through the trash and the recycling
Looking for a revolution.

I was that kid once, angry and hungry
And full of despair that told me
Things could only get better.
Me and my kind, we were all the kids
We're breaking now, bestowing on them

A world of broken things,
An empire of garbage.

Late in the afternoon, I find out
My insurance company doesn't want
To cover my prescription, because
Their suits know the bottom line
Better than my doctor knows my treatment.
In the sodden slums of my brain, I tell that kid,
"Give it a year and those suits will
Know you better than your own mother does,
Will know what you need better than you do.
At least what crumbs they're willing
To let fall to you.
Take it from an old man, whose peers
Gobble up the crumbs while you're begging for the bread."

I mourn that kid, all the kids,
Clanging, banging the heavy steel dumpster lid,
And I think a bunch of old men and women
Left that kid a heap of trash without any lunch,
Or American dream, or hope of revolution.
In the stagnant murk of early evening,
A streetlight winks on,
And a car door slams, echoing
The clanging, the relentless banging
Of Apocalypse.

WORDS ARE THE WAR

[Christopher Ropes]

"Policy" is the polite word for
"Politically-motivated murder,"
Or for progress that digs up
The bones of the ancestors
Before adding the descendants to the pile.

"Industry" is the indecisive word for
"Indigenous massacres relived,"
Or for all the years of
Cutting down trees with bulldozers
And cutting down "subhumans" with
Empty wallets, empty refrigerators, empty medicine cabinets,
And cozy little reservations
Flowing with poison and noble intentions.

"Noble intentions" is the no-balls phrase for
"No breathing room," or the way
That booze and unemployment and loneliness
Can do a race's killing for them.
Did you see the way they suffered
When the hoses were turned on them?

"Dakota Access Pipeline" is the dapper term
The dapper people use to describe
"Dappled by the Sun and rich with
Wide open spaces empty of meaningful bodies,
Where we can spread our corruption, cram it
Right down their parched and closing throats."

"White people" is the white lie
We tell ourselves when

What we mean is, "Which of you
Is like unto us? A race astride the planet,
Riding it to a lather, leaving it
Desperate in the desperate dust."
I gaze at my wicked, pale flesh,
Wishing I had the courage
To take a thirsty razor
And show "my people"
That underneath my skin,
I am the true Red Man.

COMPLICIT

[Jayaprakash Satyamurthy]

A national distraction
A national auction
Your money for your patriotism
Your hand on your heart
Feet on clouds of fervour
Head completely emptied
Cocooned by propaganda
Cushioned by heart's-talk
Robbed of all volition
A slave to wild hope
And daydreams of destiny
Craven, coward, compliant
Complicit in a conspiracy
Masquerading as a country

SILENCE MEANS DEATH
STAND ON YOUR FEET
INNER FEAR
YOUR WORST ENEMY

– Sepultura, "Refuse Resist," from *Chaos A.D.* (Roadrunner Records, 1993)

FICTION

THE LOVE PARADE

[Cody Goodfellow]

The Bleeding Hearts March For Peace was a radical pacifist blood clot, plodding up the arterial avenues of Washington, DC, on a bright, cold Valentine's Day morning, gathering mass and moving into position to stroke out the nation's brain.

Media estimates of the protesters' numbers spread from ten to forty thousand, in keeping with each outlet's bias. The organizers called it "a spontaneous and peaceful demonstration of the nation's anger," but the choreography behind it put to shame the Pentagon planners whose war they denounced. To the commuters they gridlocked, and to the pacifist army who chanted and freebased liberal outrage in its carnival ranks, it seemed like every last tree-hugging, folk-singing, granola-munching peacenik in the free world had locked arms to paralyze the nation's capitol and stop the war. To the media-eating millions, it was ugly wallpaper between talking-head gladiator-antics and the uglier war coverage.

The marchers were teachers, students, laborers, retirees, schoolchildren, housewives and veterans, who had indeed turned out to spontaneously demonstrate their anger. But in the midst of the parade, strategically scattered but linked by cryptic text messages and signs hung from windows, the hard corps of the peace movement moved and plotted.

Masked leftist cadres blocked intersections, aggravating the traffic and impeding the hundreds of cops struggling to corral the marchers, working to provoke the kind of violent crackdown that made for good TV. The Presidential Primaries were only a few weeks away, and nobody wanted trouble, so when eggs, rotten fruit and balloons filled with piss and pig blood smashed into the phalanx of plastic shields, the police stood and took it.

"Yellow," Perry growled in Don's ear. "It's like a fucking disease. Even the cops are all egg-sucking faggots, now."

In the middle of the largest body of marchers walked two men in matching green windbreakers. They could pass for father and son at a glance, and wore matching baseball caps: #1 SON and #1 DAD. They answered to Perry and Don Harlow of Petaluma, California, and had wallets filled with plausible ID. Together, they carried a big, stenciled sign that said LOVE THE WAR? ENLIST & FIGHT! LOVE THE TROOPS? BRING THEM HOME! They walked before a forty-foot puppet of Uncle Sam as the Grim Reaper waving an accusing scythe the size of a telephone pole.

When the parade turned onto Louisiana Avenue and the scrimshaw skull of the Capitol dome hove into view, Perry waved and shouted, "Treats, children!" The nearest marchers closed ranks around them and tied on bandanas and goggles.

"Help me with my backpack, son." Perry slid the bulging canvas knapsack off his shoulder and turned so Don could rummage in it. "Give 'em hell, boy."

Don took out a can and pulled the pin, lofted it high above the head of Uncle Sam. A fluffy streamer of red smoke painted an arrow to its source, but no one took notice until the can touched down. The march broke into a panicked stampede across Union Station Plaza.

Don lobbed more cans, filling each point on the compass with clouds of military-grade tear gas. The cops closed ranks and clubbed heads, leaving hogtied protesters like the spoils of a duck hunt, pushing the skirmish line away from the Capitol. Uncle Sam flopped and collapsed as his puppeteers deserted their posts. The Harlows stood fast and silently ordered the rest of their cadre to fan the flames they'd sparked to life.

Don strapped on a wet bandana, but Perry, bloodshot, weeping and flushed redder than a baboon's ass, sucked in the acrid fumes and sighed. Memories. "That's enough cover. Well begun is half done, son. Today is for real. We'll pop your cherry yet."

"Fuck you, Dad," Don croaked. "Let's get it over with."

Perry waved the cadre to their positions and jogged to catch up to a parade float that cruised on through the chaos at a stately, ocean liner pace.

The float was a papier-mache tower, a cyclopean cartoon of the President as Saturn, devouring soldiers and sailors and spouting black, oily smoke. Perry and Don crawled into the hollow base on the back of a flatbed truck.

The mechanisms that powered the President's gnashing maw and flailing arms creaked and hissed all around them. Three peaceniks stood shoulder to shoulder before a bunch of pressurized tanks connected to hoses that ran up and out the mouth of the float. A rickety picket fence of hemp fatigues, dreadlocks and flop sweat, they tried to form a wall.

Carlos, Ditto and the former leader, a poli sci grad student who called himself Spartacus on his blog, locked arms as Perry advanced on them, shouting, "Why, all of a sudden, is everyone so fucking yellow?"

Carlos pushed his glasses up his beaky nose. "We can't do this, man. There's a couple hundred school kids marching behind us."

"You loved it when it was just an idea, but you don't want peace all that bad, do you?" Perry smiled, and punched him in the gut. Carlos wilted, vomiting on his high-tops, but his comrades wouldn't budge.

Don grabbed Perry by the arm and tried to drag him back. Into Perry's hairy, wax-clotted ear, he hissed, "What the hell is this, Dad?"

"Big surprise, junior," Perry whispered, grinning so hard his dentures almost slid out. "The anti-war movement is about to grow some teeth and claws, and tear its own ass off."

The tanks had no inspection stickers. They looked like plain old oxygen, or laughing gas from the dentist, except for the blinking digital readout wired to their taps.

"Army surplus," Perry chuckled. "Tested on America's most wanted. Makes them scared, and beaucoup aggressive."

Perry had connections. It was one of the reasons he had risen to lead the cell so soon after he and Don walked into their first meeting. Chicago, '68; the Vietnam protests; Hoover's lying in state in the Capitol, in '72. He'd been fomenting chaos to bring out the ugly face of the establishment since before most of them were born. Not even Don Harlow, who had been Perry's son for eighteen months, now, knew how connected he really was.

Perry's misty yellow eyes went clear and measured Don, who flinched as if Perry really was his dad. "What, you thought these backstabbing licks of shit were gonna go fight the cops just because we threw some smoke and folk music at them?"

"I still don't get it," Don said, voice falling softer with each syllable as Perry's wrath gathered. "Why did our cell want to trash the march?"

"They're fucking traitors by nature, Don! These candy-ass radicals say they want peace, but they hate those dickless surrender-monkeys out there as much as we do. They want to play war, but they're stupid and weak. They came this far because we brought them. Because we're in charge."

Don stuck his neck in the noose. "But why are we in charge? We were just supposed to watch them."

"And there was nothing to watch, before we took over, was there? It's the bad old days, all over again.

"In the COINTELPRO ops, we got inside, but the pacifists never put down their damned dope long enough to take direct action, so, as the only ones with balls, naturally, we ended up running the show. We threw the rocks and planted the bombs, and this great nation still chokes back vomit every time they see a war protest, because of what we did. And we're going to do it again, if we have to kill every one of these gutless faggots."

Don's guts churned wet cement. This never would've happened, if they'd let him into the real FBI. "I wasn't hired to kill anybody."

"You were hired to follow orders, junior." Perry reached into his bag and almost gave him a pistol. Don could nearly hear the gear-stripped ticking of what Perry used for a brain, as he dumped it back in the sack and gave Don a gas mask, instead. "You get those tanks open, okay? I'll shoot anyone you can't get out of your way, so if you want to have a love-in later, be hard on them, now."

All Don ever wanted, was to be a good patriot. When the Army bounced him and the FBI refused even to interview him, he just kept looking for a way to serve. When he said he'd do anything, ANYTHING, to defend the United States of America from its enemies within, he truly meant it. So when he met some guys at a gun show who represented powerful patriots whose stated intent was exactly that, he eagerly signed up.

But he had no idea how much anything he could handle, until they teamed him up with Perry, whose real name Don did not ever want to know.

Don turned on the radicals, cracking his knuckles. He was big, and knew how the display of his arms limbering up worked on these scrawny vegan shitheads. Marx and Chomsky didn't teach them shit about boxing. "Open those tanks."

"Screw you, asshole." Ditto shot out a hand to push him, schoolyard-style. Don batted it aside and laid a forearm across his skull, smashing him into Carlos hard enough to stun them both. Ditto went down for the count, and Carlos, if he wasn't, was wisely faking it.

Spartacus looked around in an ecstasy of pants-pissing terror. "You're not one of us at all, are you?" His smarts only made Don eager to stomp him.

"You wanted to gas your own people," Don said, and broke his nose. "First I heard about it was just now. Do it."

"Do you know what this shit is?" Spartacus sobbed, spraying blood. "It's chemical warfare, man! Causes a huge acetylcholine spike… fight or flight reaction… makes apes go batshit and rip each other's throats out… Please…"

"I am not playing with you. Open it up."

"Or what, your dad's gonna shoot us?" Carlos raised his hands in surrender, but didn't cooperate. "Dude, my girlfriend's out there, and she's pregnant. You'll have to–"

Don was already reaching for him, but Perry got there first, with the pistol. Even with a deluxe suppressor screwed into the barrel, it looked tiny in his meaty red hand.

Perry tapped Carlos dead center in the forehead. The kid sat back against the tanks and let his last macrobiotic burrito go free-range in his hemp denim relaxed-fit jeans.

Spartacus screamed and tried to bolt, but Don tackled him, kneed him in the groin. "What did you do that for?"

Perry stepped over Spartacus, squeezed a bullet into his face without looking down. "Open the tanks, son."

Don stepped back from the hole in Carlos's head, a hole big enough he could see his whole life go swirling down it without touching the sides. "Goddamn, this is too rich for my blood."

"You're one of us, or you're one of them." Emphatically, the gun wagged at him. "Do it."

Don looked at the tanks. There was nothing like a stopcock or a simple crank to turn, but all the hoses were connected by wires to a little box with a ten-key on it.

"Code's 1968. The year we should've fucking won. We got that smartass Yankee cocksucker; we got that Red nigger rabble-rouser; we were kicking ass in Vietnam; we busted up the Democrat Convention but good; we were winning, and then it all went to shit. But we learned our lesson, boy. Punch the code in."

Don looked at the box. The last words of that egghead dipshit Spartacus rolled around in his brain. Tear each other's throats out… Please…

Thirty thousand people and a couple thousand cops, tearing each other's throats out. And he was making it happen.

If he refused, Perry would shoot him dead. In their time undercover, Don had found he didn't need to act the part of the cowed son. Perry was a natural bully, so forceful and cruel and stingy with praise, you'd forget he wasn't kin.

Don whipped around and threw the gas mask.

Perry fired, but the shot went wild. The big metal filter cone of the mask cracked the bridge of his nose and knocked his #1 DAD cap askew.

Don smashed the ten-key pad with his fist and wheeled on Perry, but the old man was already getting up, cussing, spitting blood. Don ducked and slid out from under the float, tossed his #1 SON cap into the crowd and ran.

The parade had moved through the tear gas, agitated but unbroken. Their chanting pushed out all but the sound of his heart thumping in his throat as he tried to decide what to do.

He could fade into the crowd, but where would he go? They'd hunt him down. Even if he could get away from the cops and the feds, his employers would find him and kill him. And it would still happen. Perry would get the tanks open.

Cops hemmed the parade in on both sides and massed at the corner of Constitution Avenue. He could see the sprawling greensward of the Mall up ahead. A big office building on the right faced in plate glass reflected the cold copper light of the sun into his eyes.

He ran for the cab of the truck towing the float, yanked the door open and socked the driver in the throat. The man yelped and rolled out as Don climbed in.

He stomped the gas and pumped the horn as he turned the truck hard right. The crowd split open before him, grandmothers and chubby protest warriors with toddlers in strollers dropping their signs and fleeing.

Don bounced and hit the roof hard when the truck jumped the curb, rolled over newspaper kiosks and smashed through the façade of the office building.

Metal shrieked as the ceiling peeled the float off, but the truck torpedoed the lobby and slammed into the marble-faced security desk. The steering wheel stamped his chest flat. He bit into the grubby rubber so hard his two front teeth broke off.

The engine died.

In the fleeting pocket of quiet, Don could still hear metal slamming frantically into metal.

He had to move. He couldn't move.

Perry shouted, "Hallelujah!" and a chorus of hissing, busted radiators answered him.

Don got the door open, but spilled out on his hip and screamed as his ribs grated against each other. The hissing got louder. He regretted throwing away his gas mask.

Perry jumped off the truck, stumbled with a curse and a lot of coughing, muffled by his gas mask.

Behind the truck, Don saw protestors creeping in through the shattered window, despite police who tried to push them back and get to the scene themselves.

"Get back!" he screamed. "Everybody out, there's a gas leak–"

Perry shot him in the gut. He would've got him in the face, but Don finally succeeded in pulling himself upright. The bullet punched him back two steps and bent him over, but he stayed on his feet.

"Everybody's yellow," Perry snarled, "but me."

He advanced on Don and shot him in the shoulder, which only whipped him back upright.

"Everybody balks, gets all wet at the thought of America actually winning one, and sabotages it." He raised his gun, but didn't shoot. It seemed to be very important that Don look him in the eye before he did it. It let him get that much closer.

"People like you, boy, even when you got yourself convinced you're a true blue patriot, you still sell your country down the river when the time comes. I wish I knew to do this a long time ago."

Don kept his eyes averted. He felt funny.

Where he'd been shot hurt a lot, but nowhere near what it should, for all the blood coming out of him. When he breathed, his brain tingled like it was going to sleep, but he felt lifted, like strings guided him, now. Everything was razor-sharp and vibrating, especially Perry.

The old man with the gun stood there, hyperventilating and fogging up his gas mask, toupee askew, clutching his arm against his gut. Everything tunneled down when he focused, and Perry's every physical detail swam in opalescent seas of mystical significance.

He charged.

Perry shot him almost instantly, but the bullet caromed off his skull, shearing away a divot of bone and skin and hair, but slowing him not a bit as he cross-checked Perry and tore off his mask.

The gun came up and clipped Don's jaw, knocking him back,

but he was galvanized, and almost floated on his feet. Perry turned to run, but Don caught him by his collar and spun him around.

Perry tried to hold his breath, but his face was already going purple. Don shook him until he dropped the gun, squeezed him until he gave in and took a big, deep breath.

In the confined space of the lobby, the air was totally saturated. Don could see it affecting Perry the same way it was affecting him, which was good, because he couldn't hold back any longer, and he knew, when he let go, he might never come back.

His last coherent thought was that somebody somewhere lied or fucked up big time, because since he inhaled that gas, he didn't want to kill Perry at all.

By accident or design, they sent the wrong gas. This shit was something else again, something he couldn't believe they'd do, but why cultivate anthrax or synthesize nerve gas to kill armies, when you could make an aerosolized chemical that killed war itself, by infecting the combatants with love?

He greedily soaked up the stink of hate and fear and Chesterfields and cheap bourbon that was Perry Harlow's sour spoor. He watched the darting gray tongue flick out between yellow dentures and thin, chapped lips as the old campaigner wheezed, trying to say or do something—and he wanted it, all over himself. Those watery red eyes melted in tears. The gas was making Perry feel it, too.

Don drew him closer and planted his mouth over Perry's and thrashed at that dry worm of a tongue with his own. Perry moaned into his mouth and ground his crotch into Don's thigh,

horrified and delighted to find himself with an erection for the first time in decades.

The cops surrounded them and ordered them apart, but soon succumbed to the effects of the gas, themselves. Cops and protesters went down in a crazy daisychain tangle, licking pig's blood and pepper-spray tears off each other's faces. Sobbing firemen mounted Unitarian ministers, who fellated double-amputee Vietnam vets, who in turn serviced clean-cut young congressional staffers, with beat reporters from the Times and the Post mindlessly buttonholing every anonymous source. TV newscasters and camera crews ogled the orgy until the fumes and the lovestruck hordes overwhelmed them, but the unmanned cameras rolled.

As the gas boiled out onto Louisiana Avenue and wafted across the plaza toward the Senate office buildings and the Capitol Dome, hundreds of rescue workers and police and marchers rushed to the scene, only to tear off their own and each other's clothes, and joined the cavorting hordes in discovering a new true spirit of the holiday.

Though the news never mentioned Don and Perry Barlow by their real or assumed names, the message spread with viral speed around the globe. Sheer sensationalism put the story live on every screen in the free world, and even totalitarian states could not resist dropping the veil for a moment to show their subjects the depravity of America. Soldiers and politicians everywhere were stunned to silence, then broke out in righteous indignation or riotous laughter. And for a day here, a moment there, there was no war. ∎

BLOOD AND THUNDER

[Dominique Lamssies]

Nathan bounced in his chair at the dinner table. His older sister Gina set down a plate of garlic bread and the little boy snatched a piece and shoved it in his mouth like he was starving.

"If you keep eating bread you won't be able to fit anything else in your belly," Gina teased, ruffling his brown hair as she sat down.

Their mother, Beth, set down a bowl of pasta. Nathan shouted something that they thought was the word "spaghetti" and sent soggy bread crumbs flying all over the table.

"Jeez, Nathan. Not with your mouth full." Beth frowned as she scooped noodles onto his plate.

The boy smiled so big it squeezed his eyes closed as he chewed. Gina giggled as she tied back the long blonde hair she'd inherited from her mother.

"Good choice, Nathan. This will hit the spot," his father, Peter, said with a warm smile. He was slightly too tall for the table so he leaned down as he lifted his fork to make sure nothing got on his shirt.

"I'm glad someone knew what they wanted," Beth said as she passed the bowl to Gina. "We'd have been arguing all night if someone hadn't been decisive."

Gina let out a disgusted sigh and glared at her mom as she flipped pasta onto her plate so hard the splat was audible. Peter deliberately looked away from his wife and smiled at Gina as she passed him the bowl.

Beth's eyes moved back and forth between her plate and her husband, hoping Peter would take the bait but he didn't.

A knock on the front door cut the tension. Peter stood and made an effort not to look at anyone as he went to answer it.

On the other side of the door was a man who had obviously been in a fight. His brown hair was disheveled, his clothes were shredded and his face had red welts all over it. It crossed Peter's mind that the man was on the thin and scrawny side and probably would have been on the losing end of just about any fight.

"Sorry to disturb you, but I got mugged up the street," the man said with a shy smile. "They took my wallet and phone. Do you mind if I use yours?"

Peter's brow creased. Mugged? In this neighborhood? That had never happened in the twenty years he and Beth had been living there.

"Mind if I come in?" the man asked and smiled wide.

Peter found himself staring at the man's very white teeth and forgot what he'd been so concerned about.

"Sure," Peter said. He went to the table in the entryway and unplugged his work phone from the charger.

The man stared out the door for a moment as if he were searching for something before he closed it.

Peter handed him the phone. The man thanked him. Peter walked back to the dining room.

Nathan was peeking out, watching the man. Peter nudged him back to the table and cringed a bit. Why did everything suddenly smell like basil?

"What is it?" Beth asked.

"A guy was mugged up the street. He's using our phone to call the police."

"Mugged?" Beth challenged. She frowned and looked at him sidelong as she twisted her fork into a pasta nest. "I hope you didn't invite him in because he's lying. No one gets mugged around here."

Peter stared at his wife. He hated it when she tried to bait him into a fight. He wouldn't give her the satisfaction. Not in front of the kids, at least.

Gina let out another giant sigh. "Jesus, Mom, how much basil did you put in this? I can't taste anything else," she whined and looked sidelong at her mother, hoping to push her buttons.

Normally it would have worked but this time Beth frowned. "I didn't put any basil in it. I hate basil. Where is that coming from?" She craned her neck to look over the bread.

"He didn't dial the phone," Nathan blurted out.

Everyone stopped.

"What?" Peter asked.

"You can't call the police when you don't dial the phone," the boy said matter-of-factly, then ate some noodles.

Peter looked back into the hall.

The man had the phone to his ear and his back to Peter. He was mumbling something Peter couldn't make out.

Beth was right. No one got mugged in their neighborhood. That guy had probably passed a cop car to get there.

"Stay here," he told the rest of his family as he approached the man. He cringed a little. The basil smell was in the hallway too.

"You spoke to the police?" he asked as the man hung up.

"I did, yes. Thank you," the man said with that smile again.

This time it annoyed Peter.

"You didn't ask for our address. That means the police won't know where to find you," Peter said as he took his phone.

"I described the place it happened," the man said, looking like he had been caught in a lie. His cheek muscles strained as if he were trying to smile bigger.

Peter pulled up the call history on the phone. No one had made a call on it since he'd left work two hours ago. He looked back up at the man.

"Get out before I really call the cops."

The man's eyes were confused, but he kept smiling. He held his hands up. "Look, the people who mugged me are still out there,"

"Which means you're endangering my family." Peter took a step forward. "Get out."

The man backed up. "All I need is a few minutes to make a plan and then I'll be out of your hair."

"Get… out," Peter repeated. He opened the door with one hand and put his other on the man's shoulder, ready to shove him out. Peter wasn't the brawniest guy, but he was bigger than the man.

They saw a little book on the doorstep. Peter looked confused. He reached down to pick it up.

The man grabbed Peter's shoulder and jerked him back, slamming the door. The breeze the door pulled in as it shut reeked of basil.

Peter thrust a hand at the door. "It said Gospel of St. John. It was just a flier some religious nut left."

The man grabbed Peter's arm and yanked him toward the dining room. The phone slipped out of Peter's hand.

"Where's the backdoor?" the man demanded.

"Wh… what?" Peter sputtered. He tried to pull his arm away, but the man's grip was too strong.

In the dining room, the man let go of Peter and looked over the rest of the family.

"Where is the backdoor?" he repeated.

Nathan slid from his chair and sidled over to his sister, who wrapped a protective arm around him.

Beth shot to her feet. "What the hell is going on?"

"Do you not speak English!" he shouted her down.

Rage seized the woman's face and her mouth opened. The man pinched his thumb and index finger together and slid them to the side as if he were zipping something shut. Beth's mouth closed and she wasn't sure why.

"I am going to take you to the backdoor," he explained in a level voice, "where you will exit this house. Whatever happens to me after that will not be your problem, understood?"

"Okay," she said. "The backdoor is through the kitchen."

The man stormed off.

Gina looked at her mom and dad, confusion wrinkling her forehead. Peter opened his mouth to reassure her but Beth grabbed his arm so tight it hurt.

"We don't want to be trapped in the house with him," she whispered. "We'll go outside and call the police."

Peter gritted his teeth, trying not to get angry that Beth wouldn't let him talk.

The family moved into the kitchen together. Peter shook off his wife's hand with a glare. Gina positioned herself in front of Nathan.

The man had his hand on the doorknob. "Thanks for joining me. And I wouldn't bother calling the cops. It won't do any good." He yanked the door open.

A dagger had been driven into the porch, right at the edge of the doorjamb.

"Fuck," the man hissed.

"What is that?" Beth asked.

Gina narrowed her eyes and moved directly behind the man. She could just shove him out the door. Her parents were close enough to shut it behind him.

"An iron dagger," the man said with a grimace.

"How do you know it's iron?" Beth snapped, her hands going to her hips.

A gun fired from the darkness beyond the open door.

The man screamed and his hand shot to his collarbone. He kicked the door closed and ducked aside, out of sight of the windows.

"Gina!" Nathan screamed at the top of his lungs.

Peter and Beth turned.

Gina was laying on the floor. The gelatinous remains of her right eye were dribbling down her temple. Her mouth opened and closed as if she were trying to say something. Blood pooled under her head.

The boy collapsed next to his sister. "Someone help her! She's going to die!" He threw himself on her chest, sobbing.

"Is there another way out of the house?" the man shouted, trying to drown out the child.

"You piece of crap!" Peter cried. "My daughter was just shot and you're still trying to save yourself?"

The man rolled his eyes as if Peter was the stupidest person he'd ever met.

"If there's another way out then you can get her help."

"Get her help!" Nathan howled.

"Oh for crap's sake, everybody upstairs," the man commanded. He reached down, grabbed the boy's arm and tried to pull him away. Nathan shrieked and instantly started fighting, his sister's name punctuating the ruckus.

Beth hollered, "let him go!" and wrenched the boy away. Peter shoved the man against the wall.

"You need to tell us what is going on," he growled.

"You need to tell me where another exit is," the man growled back.

"That is quite useless," a woman's voice came from the backdoor that she had opened during the row. It was a redhead in black with a gun trained on the man. "I've got all the exits covered with cold iron. Iron bullets too. That's why that wound hurts so much," she said, a hint of glee in her voice.

"That's also why it went straight through me and hit her. You doused the house in basil oil too," he sneered.

"I need them clear headed," she asserted.

"Who are you!" Peter shouted, waving his hands about in frustration. He wasn't sure which was worse, the destruction they were causing or the fact that neither of them noticed the effect it was having on his family.

The woman shook the gun in their direction.

"Tell them," she commanded.

The man's eyes narrowed and his free hand started fidgeting.

"You're the one who shot their daughter. You tell them," he spat petulantly.

She fired at his jittery hand, barely missing it.

"Don't," she warned him, then said to everyone else, "you are harboring a witch. I don't know why and I don't care. But I will kill him. You will step aside and let me handle this or there will be consequences."

Beth was livid. "You fucking shot my daughter because you think this dumb ass is a witch!" she cried.

"Yes," the woman stated.

"You're the psycho with the gun! You're the only dangerous one I see here!"

The woman ignored her.

"You have fifteen minutes. If I don't come out with his body, my associates will set fire to this house. You will help me, or you will suffer the consequences. Those are your choices."

Peter and Beth glanced at each other.

"You think they have any say in this?" the man asked, trying very hard to look intimidating.

"They do. It's just like your kind to think you're better than us, that we can't do anything against you." A mirthless smile spread across her face. "You'll see what we can do to you. And you'll regret your arrogance."

Nathan shot to his feet and ran at the woman with a wail. He threw himself at her torso but he was so slight he barely made an impact.

"You hurt Gina!" he screamed, his fists flailing at her. "You hurt her! Make her better!"

The woman raised an eyebrow, sneered and struck the child across the face with the back of her hand.

Beth started toward the child but stopped short when the woman pulled another gun and pointed it at her.

"You should have taught your brat better manners."

"And you should focus on your real opponent," the man said. He flung out the hand that had been pressed to his wound, splattering blood around.

"Shit," the woman snapped. Her eyes roved for a moment as she surveyed the room and calculated. Then she took off past them into the hallway.

The blood drops were spreading into pools on their own, even where they hit the wall.

Nathan was the only one who didn't notice. His red, tear-stained face was focused on the woman. He wanted to hurt her for what she'd done to Gina. He ran after her as she stopped near the front door.

But something darted in front of him. Long, thin, knobby legs shoved him to the floor to get to the woman. He saw what looked like the head of a hyena with six legs protruding from where its neck should have been. Each leg had a nasty looking claw on the end. The collision annoyed the thing enough that it turned on the boy. It growled at him, lowering its head to look him over.

"Nathan, don't move," Peter called, started to creep down the hall.

But Nathan screamed and kicked out with both legs, nailing the creature where the legs joined the neck.

It staggered back and righted itself. The man whistled, striding into the hall with more of the creatures. The thing stood at attention.

Nathan panicked and ran for the stairs to the second floor. Both parents shouted for him and rushed forward, but had to dodge the half dozen creatures that had arrayed themselves against the woman. The shooting started when they reached the bottom of the stairs. They ran as fast as they could and

barely stopped to breath once they'd reached the top. Peter charged toward Nathan's room and opened the door. The boy wasn't there.

"How could you have dropped your phone down there?" Beth snapped as she charged into the bedroom for hers.

Peter followed. "Like I was supposed to magically know the guy was going to bring a gun wielding maniac into our house."

She leveled a venomous glare at him. "You were the one who let him in. The first time in two years you actually make a decision and it's the wrong one."

"Are you fucking kidding me, Beth? Are you really blaming me for this?"

She turned her back on him and spoke into the phone. "Yes, there are two intruders in my house and one of them has shot my daughter."

Peter stormed out into the hall. The noise below had settled into a din that sounded like thunder. He pressed his hands to his ears to block it out but it didn't work. There was a crack so loud it shook the entire house.

Someone in Gina's room screamed.

Peter ran to the door and threw it open. Beth dropped the phone and followed.

There was a gaping hole in the middle of the room. The edges were warping downward in a steady motion. The thunder of gunfire was accompanied by splintering wood as the floor bent and twisted, reaching down into the living room below.

Nathan was clutching one edge, looking about frantically for a piece of furniture to grab onto, but the motion of the spiral kept moving everything just out of reach.

"Daddy!" the boy begged.

"I'm coming," his father assured him and moved forward cautiously.

As he got near the hole he saw the man below, his arms extended in front of him. He was directing the warped wood as if it were a shield. Shots from the other side tore through the wood and even though they didn't hit the man, he was flinching as if they did.

The shooting stopped. The man looked up and said, "she's reloading. Take the boy and go."

"Daddy!" Nathan cried again

"The witch has endangered your son," the woman shouted from the other side of the battered wooden wall. "Will you still defend him?"

Peter leaned down and grabbed his son's arm. He pulled the boy up and hugged him.

"If you weren't trying to kill him, he wouldn't be endangering us," he shouted back as his son trembled against him. Beth moved up behind him and tried to grab Nathan, but Peter hugged the weeping boy harder.

"You selfish prick," she muttered.

The woman downstairs clicked her tongue so loud they could all hear it. "You are weak. You believe his lies. Now it will cost you your son."

There was a sound like a chicken leg being pulled from its carcass. The witch screamed and floor of the bedroom shuddered, sending father and son tumbling to the living room below.

Nathan panicked again and struggled out of his father's arms as they fell. He landed on his side and there was a snap his father knew was a bone breaking. The boy wailed.

Peter impacted on his back but managed to keep his head from hitting.

He saw the woman cutting through the wall with a wooden knife and he didn't understand why that should work, let alone why it seemed to be hurting the man so much.

She glanced at Peter as she worked at the wood. "You'll thank me for this later," she said with a surety Peter couldn't fathom anymore than anything else going on around him.

Nathan squealed and Peter looked back to see that one of the creatures had jabbed a clawed foot into the boy's leg and was dragging him off.

Beth was running down the stairs, trying not to cry when the shooting started again. Nothing that was happening made sense. It had all spiraled out of control so fast, and there was no way to get it back under control.

When she reached the living room, the wood shield was starting to crumble.

The tearing sound came again as the woman cut out part of the wall and a gash opened up in the man's chest.

"I love Rowan wood." The woman seemed to be gloating. "It shouldn't cut a thing, but when you pit it against witch magic,"

A creature jumped through the newly created hole, cutting her off mid-sentence.

Beth saw that there were only two creatures left. The other one was keeping her son trapped in the corner. The boy cowered, clutching his arm. The fight had finally been terrified out of him.

Beth slipped into the living room and cleared off a small side table without making any noise. She lifted the table by the legs and turned to the man.

Peter stood and grabbed hold of the tabletop. "What are you doing?" he asked softly, glad the shooting had started again so the man wouldn't notice them.

Beth clinched her jaw. "If he hadn't come here, she wouldn't be doing this. She'll leave when she has him," she growled.

"Are you crazy?" Peter scoffed. "She's the nut job trying to kill him. He's just defending himself."

"You would side with the one who does what he wants and doesn't care about anyone else," she spat. She tried to pull the table from his grasp but he wouldn't let go.

"You're the one so blinded by your anger that you can't see straight," he countered.

She shoved the table at him hard enough to fling him back. She swung the table with all her might at the witch's back. It shattered against him. So did the wooden wall.

The creature behind Beth scurried forward. It slashed at her and tried to bite her, forcing her backward. Once her back was to a bookcase it jammed its claws into her upper arms and held her there.

The woman finally managed to put a bullet in the creature's brain when the fire alarm in the hallway went off.

The redhead looked about as bad as the witch did. She had several open wounds and was struggling to breath, but she didn't hesitate. She lunged forward and stabbed the man in the chest with her wooden knife. He roared as he grabbed her by the throat and charged, slamming her into the wall.

"Afraid to die, witch?" she choked out.

"You're the one dying today," he hissed. He gave a wicked smile as he pried her mouth open with one hand. He wedged his fingers where the lips met the gums under her nose and pushed, forcing skin off bone as his fingers worked their way under her cheek.

The woman screamed and thrashed in his grip. But she wasn't lashing out. She was trying to get loose while she fought to get something from her jacket. She pulled out a vial of something dark purple and squeezed her hand around it. It broke in her fist. She opened her palm just long enough to ram it into his chest.

He screamed and jerked back, ripping his hand away and leaving a sagging, ragged flap of skin on the right side of the woman's face that gushed blood down her neck.

But she laughed and blood bubbled and sputtered out of the limp side of her mouth.

"Bless your witch's allergy to elderberry," she cackled.

Peter moved slowly and quietly over to his son, not wanting to draw anyone's attention. He hugged the boy again and looked around the room. The pair was fighting near the door, so he would risk putting Nathan in the line of fire if he went that way. Smoke was starting to pour in from the hallway to the kitchen, which meant the fire was that way. He could try to break a window, but that could mean more and worse injuries to both he and his son. Not to mention there was still one of those creatures that might come after him if he tried to escape and the woman's associates who might attack them once they got outside. He began breathing heavily, fighting to keep the helplessness at bay. He watched the fight, trying desperately to find a way out.

The woman sprung forward, blade out, and caught the man's throat with it. He rushed at her again and slammed her into the wall with his full weight. She hit so hard it left an indent. She slid to the floor, out cold. The man put a hand to his throat as if that would staunch the bleeding. He turned to Peter.

"You." He pointed to the front door. "Get rid of that Gospel of St. John on the doorstep."

Peter moved in front of Nathan. "Go fuck yourself."

The man reached out with his free hand, grabbed a vase on the table next to him and shattered it against the edge. His bloody hand pointed to the boy. Nathan yelped as an invisible force dragged him away so fast Peter couldn't catch him.

The man put the jagged edge of the vase to the boy's face.

"Move… the book."

Peter got to his feet and went straight to the door. He picked up the little book and threw it as far as he could toward the street.

The man pushed the boy away and dropped the remains of the vase. He walked backward out the door and Peter thought he saw regret in the man's eyes for the first time.

"I'm sorry you got caught in the middle of this. I really am," he said as he passed over the threshold. "But some people can't be reasoned with. They can't see beyond their hatred and they will do anything to preserve what isn't worth preserving." He turned and staggered out of sight.

Peter coughed, suddenly realizing how much smoke there was in the air. He looked at his son.

"Listen, honey, I need you to run to Mrs. Parker next door, okay? You'll be safe there."

But Nathan looked panicked.

"No! Daddy!" he cried.

A boot connected with Peter's back, sending him to the floor. He rolled over and saw the woman, her eyes wild with rage. She punched him in the face and his head cracked against the floor. She punched him twice more as if she were venting some pent up rage.

"Stop!" Nathan begged. "Don't hurt my Daddy!"

"It's scum like you that let this scourge continue." She clamped both hands on his throat and squeezed. She lowered her face to his. Blood from her face dripped on him.

"The rats will never defend you. They're just waiting to feast on your carcass. You need us." She reached out and grabbed the broken vase. She stabbed it into his side. "People like you deserve whatever you get." She stood, spat on him and walked out the door to follow the trail of blood the witch had left behind.

Peter stared at the ceiling, the pain so great all he could focus on was the smoke thickening above him. Nathan sat beside him, crying so hard he couldn't get any words out.

Peter started to reach for the boy, but Beth materialized behind him and pulled the child away.

"You saw her," Peter whispered. "You saw her come at me and you didn't say anything."

"Yeah," Beth nodded, "and you didn't come help me when that thing had me. So fuck you too." She pushed the boy away and they left his view.

Peter heard an ambulance siren. He pulled the glass from his stomach and felt blood gush under his hand. After the first wave of pain passed he flipped over, forcing himself to crawl onto the porch.

Beth and Nathan had stopped near the street. Nathan was waving a hand in his direction and shouting something.

Beth looked at her husband with nothing but hatred. Peter could feel the same hatred in his own eyes as he looked back at his wife. He sagged against the porch. The ambulance was probably too late for Gina. Hopefully it would be too late for him. If he woke up tomorrow, he'd have to face all the ugly things he and his wife had learned about each other tonight. Gina wouldn't have to go through it and he was glad. Dying would be a thousand times easier than that. ■

EVERY LITTLE SOUL MUST SHINE

[Eric Schaller]

"You're killing me," Daniel cried. He was sick with anger.

Melody trembled and said nothing. Then, very purposely, she turned to look out the window at Lake Waubesa. It was the fourth of July and a few boats puttered about enjoying the remnants of the warm summer day. Mosquitoes would soon be out. Fireworks were scheduled for later that evening.

"Did you hear one single thing I said?"

Melody's shoulders tightened but she refused to answer.

Daniel grabbed her shoulder. The very least she could do was to look him in the eyes.

She almost spat in his face. "Don't you ever do that to me," she said. "Don't you ever lay a hand on me."

★★★★★

On a hot, sweaty day in August, a Saturday marred only by the prediction of evening thunderstorms, Daniel took a bus to Middleton and disembarked at its westernmost stop. His destination was a spot on the map named Festge Park, out past Cross Plains and about eight miles distant. Tramping along the marge of the highway, backpack cinched and already cutting into his shoulders, Daniel witnessed the rapid transition of city into farmland, undulating fields of corn that extended into a gray-green, dusty blur, punctuated by occasional trees and houses. The cornfields rippled in a breeze he did not feel. Turkey buzzards rode the thermals. He wore a baseball cap but his eyes stung from dribbling sunscreen. He blinked. He wiped his eyes and forehead free of sweat. He blinked some more.

A smell, sick and fruity and instantly recognizable, distracted him. A dead groundhog on its back, limbs almost absorbed into its bloated torso, head glued to the asphalt by a dried mass of brains and tarry blood. Flies buzzed and crawled, bejeweling the suppurating carcass. A little further down the road he came upon a dead squirrel and then, not that he was keeping tally, a rabbit, a porcupine, another dead squirrel, the crumpled remains of a hawk, and another groundhog. All within the space of a mile. The depressing number of the dead was multiplied a thousand, a million-fold across the highways and byways of America. Barely had the stench of the last groundhog dissipated but it was replaced by that of a dead possum, its hair dingy, its rear legs crushed, the bloody fur, flesh, and bone jammed into indentations of the asphalt rumble strip. Had someone purposely swerved to hit the poor bumbling creature?

A car screamed by and Daniel jerked to attention. Overburdened by his backpack, he almost toppled to the pavement. The kids inside yelled the gibberish of assholes everywhere and one threw a soda can. It missed and skipped across the pavement to lodge in the crabgrass. Cola dregs burbled forth. It was past eleven o'clock and off to his left, protruding from the oceanic fields of corn was a forested hill that suggested cool respite from the oppressive sun and the bloody trail of death. It was still early enough in Daniel's pilgrimage for him to consider a deviation from his route. Besides, it was almost lunchtime.

★★★★★

A circuitous thirty minutes later, crouched beneath the buzzing wires of a powerline, Daniel pawed through the pockets of his backpack. He found his bottle of DEET insect repellent, the travel flask he had painstakingly filled with Wild Turkey 101 bourbon, and the lone cigar that Professor Hausmann had given him that past Thursday. "You'll figure it out," Hausmann had said, "I have faith in you." This all in relation to Daniel's biochemistry studies which seemed to be going nowhere. It was year five into his Ph.D. and he could foresee nothing changing for years six, seven, eight, and so on. Hausmann had handed Daniel a cigar because he'd just had his first baby and had a celebratory surplus. "You should relax," he said.

That had been one impetus for Daniel's solo hike.

His month-old breakup with Melody was the other.

Daniel needed time away from all distractions: friends, phone, internet. He needed to get back to basics, the simple necessities of food and shelter, what you could carry on your back, muscles aching, blood pumping, an antidote for too many weeks standing at a lab bench.

He found the bag with his sandwiches stuffed in a pack pocket intended for a water bottle. He spread the bag on a humped boulder, his two sandwiches on top, his camping equivalent to table, placemat, and plateful of food. A blackberry bush grew nearby but the fruit he tasted was desiccated, past peak. He swigged warm water flavored with plastic from his Nalgene bottle. He probably hadn't been drinking enough. There was a danger of dehydration, of heat stroke. He salivated like a famished dog at the first bite of his sandwich: cheddar, salami, and briny pickle slices.

He'd discovered a very boring, very recent housing development on top of the emerald hill, one dedicated to estates of the rich and wanna-be-famous. "Excessive roofline," is how Melody would have phrased it. She had an enviable way of condensing complex concepts into sound bites. There was a two-lane dirt trail for maintenance running beneath the power line, a shortcut back to his original route. It also served as a convenient no man's land for lunch away from those greedy houses with their manicured lawns. His view took in the patchwork cornfields, the low-slung town of Cross Plains, and beyond that, shadowed by a few storm clouds and obscured by dancing heat waves, the distant bluff of Festge Park.

"Hello." A voice announced itself from behind Daniel. There was an edge to the voice, a desire to make itself known before its owner approached too closely. "Do you live here?"

Daniel lowered his sandwich.

His interrogator was in his mid-forties. He wore jeans along with a button shirt, the sleeves rolled just shy of his elbows. He hadn't shaved but it was a weekend growth destined to disappear come Monday. "Do you live here?" He was going to repeat himself until he got an answer.

"Just passing through. I thought this was a nice place to have lunch." Daniel gestured at the view. "It's beautiful up here."

"That's why we live here." The man smiled but did not move closer. He had soft hands and he pressed his fingertips together for emphasis. "What's your name?"

"Daniel."

"Well, Daniel, it's nice to meet you." The man shoved his hands into the pockets of his jeans, knuckles outlined against the tasteful denim. "This isn't your home," he said as if stating a simple fact.

"I just stopped here for lunch."

"This is private property."

It was well past the point where Daniel could have explained he was a graduate student at the University of Wisconsin. Filthy jeans, pitted blue t-shirt, and dusty backpack, he looked like a vagrant. He even felt pride in his appearance as if he embodied a character out of Steinbeck, as if he had earned the saintly anger of a bum confronted by the privilege of wealth. "I'm not bothering anybody. I'm just eating my lunch."

"But you are bothering us. You don't belong here."

Daniel slapped the rock that served as his table. "This belongs to the power company, not you."

The man regarded Daniel in silence.

Daniel wanted to outwait that silence but patience was not his strong suit. "I'm not doing anything wrong, anyway."

"We don't want any trouble."

"I'm not trying to give anybody any trouble. I just want to eat my lunch." The argument was going around in circles.

"Maybe you'd like to discuss this with my neighbor," the man said. "He's with the MPD."

"MPD?"

"Middleton Police Department."

Daniel's cheeks prickled. "Can't I even finish my lunch?"

"I'd prefer not."

Daniel sighed. "Let me get my stuff together." He slowly, methodically returned everything he had extracted from his pack to its rightful place. He hoped the man recognized that he was stretching out the time it took to accomplish a simple task. He hoped that it pissed the man off. His adversary smiled as if listening to a tune only he could hear.

Daniel hoped the man was seething inside.

Daniel braced his pack on the rock table, crouched in front of it, feeling comically exposed, and slipped his arms through the straps. He rose, hefted its weight. It was heavier than he remembered and it hurt in all the familiar places. He cinched the waist belt and shuffled around to face his antagonist. "Okay, I'm off."

The man nodded. "Good bye, Daniel."

"What's your name? Not that I'm ever coming back here."

"Gerald." The man didn't offer his last name.

"Good to meet you, Gerald. No, great to meet you."

"Good luck with your travels," Gerald said as if bidding fare-thee-well to a houseguest.

Daniel thought of saying more and searched his mind for one last cutting remark. It wasn't worth it. He still had six hard miles to Festge Park and the distant bellying clouds didn't promise safe passage. He hoped the thunderstorm would hold off until he had set up camp.

★★★★★

Daniel had descended only a little way down the scrubby path—he was looking for more blackberries, he was thinking about an erotic photograph in Melody's bedroom, an art shot of her supine and naked torso, her back arched, providence of a former boyfriend who had his own darkroom, who she still remained friends with—when Gerald called out after him, "Give my regards to the goatman." That's what it sounded like but a cracking rip of thunder obscured the last part. Daniel missed a step, stumbling beneath the weight of his pack. Thunder but no rain, as yet. He was embarrassed by this show of weakness and didn't turn to respond to Gerald's cry. He didn't want to give that asshole any extra satisfaction. He trudged step by step down the hill until he reached the highway and resumed his pilgrimage.

★★★★★

The laughter of picnickers caught up in the spell of late summer. The smell of grilled hamburgers dripping fat onto charcoal. Daniel plodded past it all, invisible in his isolation. There was a sumac colony beyond the park shelter, beyond the playfield with its slack badminton net and the abandoned rackets. The fuzzy red spires of the trees thrust toward the clouds. Melody had once used sumac fruit to make a drink. Indian lemonade, she called it. She mashed the ruddy fruit, steeped it in cold water, and then strained the liquid into a glass with sugar. Much too tart and Daniel spat his mouthful into the sink. Melody laughed at his puckered expression and licked the residue from his lips. Kissed him. That had been one of their happier moments.

Poison ivy and brambles grew beneath the sumacs, but there were also paths, maybe trod by animals, maybe by kids sneaking off to smoke weed. Daniel needed a secluded spot for the night—Festge Park closed at sundown, no camping allowed—and he ducked under the spindly branches. Twigs scraped his pack. Someone had lost a blue Frisbee and there was trash everywhere. A basketball sneaker missing laces, a McDonald's bag, a rotted towel, some wadded toilet paper. It'd be just his luck to step in somebody's shit.

He emerged from the corrupted grove onto a lip of rock that overlooked an oak and hickory forested slope. He saw the highway he'd tramped along for those long sweaty miles and, on the other side, spied something he'd missed earlier: an opalesque pond fringed by thickly growing trees. It would have the wait. The beaten path circled down and around the limestone bluff, and he was soon enveloped in the green silence afforded by the muffling leaves. A relative silence, new sounds coming to the fore. The morbid cry of a crow, the whine of a bloodthirsty mosquito.

The path dipped and looped and brought him up against an earthen wall riddled with twisted roots, an immense oak ripped from its footing by a windstorm. The oak was partly dead and partly alive, just enough roots remaining to sustain its thin new growth that pushed upward past the lichen-encrusted wood. Someone had hung an emptied bottle of Leinenkugel beer from a protruding root at eye level. Daniel skirted the exposed root mass and discovered a stretch of level ground and a graffiti-scarred concavity in the outcropping behind it. He dropped his backpack and gave silent thanks to those benefactors who had beaten the path to this secluded spot, a perfect pitch for his tent.

He sucked at the warm remnants in his water bottle and examined the graffiti after setting up camp. There were satanic symbols and crude phrases, some writings eroded into indecipherability. All of it, the ancient and the modern, was scratched into the rock. No spray paint, as if the modern-day perpetrators maintained a tradition established by their spiritual forefathers. Daniel had the uneasy feeling he was looking back into time, at a ceremony of delinquency that had the seal of history's approval. The most impressive piece, the work of a true artist, degenerate or not, was a satanic face topped by immense antlers, these so intricate, so interlaced that they mirrored the branches of the forest. Someone who lacked the artist's touch had scratched a name below the bas-relief: GOATMAN.

★ ★ ★ ★ ★

"You're killing me." Daniel had screamed these words at Melody a little over a month ago, on the fourth of July. They were arguing and she misinterpreted everything he said. She turned her back on him and he grabbed her shoulder, just to get her to listen, but she almost spat in his face. "Don't you ever do that to me," she said. "Don't you ever lay a hand on me." What was he supposed to do? What could he do? He stormed out of her house. "You're killing me," he cried and slammed the door behind him. She lived that summer on the forested shore of Lake Waubesa, house-sitting for friends who were gone gathering ancestral strains of maize in Mexico. He stalked the lakeshore trail. He didn't see or remember anything along the way, just ran over what he said and she said again and again in his mind, obsessing. None of it made any sense.

He thought of that argument again now, that same old argument about commitment and her desire to have a baby, as he circled Salmo Pond. That was the name of the jewel-like pond he had seen from the vantage of Festge Park. There had

been a few cars in the parking lot but no one on the trail, the weekend warriors driven off by the approach of rain. Daniel's legs and shoulders were sore but he felt strangely buoyant now that he no longer carried his pack. He'd tidied up in a park bathroom and his wet hair, slicked behind his ears, cooled in the twilight breeze.

He took out the celebratory cigar that Hausmann had gifted him. He lit it and inhaled the savory smoke. He tasted apples and pumpkin pie, autumn smells rich with nostalgia, with the sense of time passing, of opportunities lost. He cursed himself. Nostalgia was a cop-out and he resolved to enjoy, to experience each day as it came. Just then he passed the pungent refuse of a fisherman who'd scaled and cleaned his fish before heading home. Maybe there was no law against such waste, but there should be. He paused. Something about the location was familiar. The small pond, ringed by trees, its encircling trail and the offshoots that led into secluded copses. What did Salmo mean? Something about fish, something maybe that Melody had told him.

Christ!

Was there no escape? Did everything in his life circle back to the same damned thing?

Melody had mentioned Salmo Pond and he had asked her a question as to its meaning. She had not known but instead told him about her former boyfriend, Toby, someone he had never met but still felt he knew too much about. Toby was the source of the erotic photograph Melody still kept on the wall in her bedroom. "We had sex there," she said. She then proceeded to describe how she and Toby had walked the circular trail. They'd discussed fishing technique with the folks they encountered and then, at the far end of the pond, followed a trail into the trees. "I was wearing a dress but no underwear," she said. She giggled. "The game warden found us. He was checking for fishing licenses. Toby tried to stuff himself back into his pants but he couldn't make it fit. I dropped my skirt but not before the warden got an eyeful."

Maybe that story had been an invitation. Not long afterward, Melody had tried to convince Daniel to drive her across town to her old high school. "Why?" he asked. "I've got some business there," she said. That was no answer and Daniel repeated his question. "I'll make it worth your while," she said. She licked her upper lip and curled her tongue. Was this to be a new erotic adventure? Or was Daniel simply a stand-in for one of his predecessors? He didn't have the guts to ask. Melody got angry when he said there was no way he was going to risk being discovered by some pimpled kids with his pants down.

He inhaled the smoke from his cigar, too deeply. The burn spread into his lungs and he coughed. Rain began to fall, sporadic drops that hammered at his skin, insistent, their coolness spreading into his flesh. Dust cratered at his feet and the smell of rain rose like a fog. He thought again about the erotic photograph Melody kept in her bedroom, the way the light caught the patch of pubic hair visible behind her upraised thigh.

"You're killing me," he'd screamed at the top of his lungs and slammed the door. "You're killing me." How could anyone ignore that? Yet, when he returned to the house an hour later, Melody was calm as could be, her clothes changed, and a blanket, a bottle of merlot, and wineglasses—"I won't drink wine from a plastic cup"—packed into a promotional knapsack she'd received at a maize conference. "Hurry," she said, "I don't want to miss the fireworks." They listened to the radio on the drive to Warner Park, stars perforating the blackening sky. Melody said something about anger and love being two sides of the same emotional coin. She kissed him just to remind him of what he was missing. Daniel was skeptical of her logic but he knew enough not to argue. The radio played "4th of July" by the band X.

★★★★★

The Goatman.

Rain splattered in thunderous drops against Daniel's tent. The nylon rebounded like the skin on a tambourine. He huddled in the middle of the tent, legs drawn up, knees bound behind his forearms like a stupid Christmas elf. He was afraid to brush the ceiling because that might elicit a never-ending trickle of water. He was afraid to step beyond the rectangle of his sleeping pad because there was a lagoon trapped between the underlying tarp and the tent.

There was also the Goatman. Daniel had situated the zippered entrance to his tent facing away from the bluff. This was a precaution, an insurance that no one could sneak up on him. But now he wondered about the graffiti scratched into the rock behind and invisible to him. The repeated motifs of the five-pointed star, the ludicrous 666, the demonic phrases, the protruding features of that leering sculpture with its antlers. Those terribly elongated antlers. He felt their points in his back.

He spun around but there was nothing there.

He'd heard the tale of the Goatman almost every summer since he'd arrived in Madison, invariably while he and his friends were sitting around a campfire. The last time had been in Kettle Moraine State Park, everyone so drunk the stars were spinning. The tale was an obvious predecessor to that modern-day classic, the man with the hook who terrorizes a couple fooling around in their car. But the tale of the Goatman was purportedly from the Civil War era. The horse-drawn wagon of a virginal bride and her husband breaks down on a desolate road, the husband goes for help, and in his absence a hairy goat-like creature appears to terrorize the bride. The beast's smell is enough to gag a corpse and the air buzzes with hungry flies. The bride cowers in the wagon. Hours later, after the monster abandons the locale, the bride runs off in search of her husband, only to find his bloodied body hanging from a tree, hoof prints in the trampled mud.

A disturbance outside the tent. Just a flicker of lightning in the distance?

Lightning cracked again and the elongated shadows of branches stretched across his tent, intricate, interlaced like antlers extended out beyond…beyond what? A skull-rattling roll of thunder. Beyond the periphery of Daniel's tent and into demonic infinity.

He was scaring himself.

There was nothing out there, nothing but the dance of elements. A thunderstorm at night. Daniel dabbed a kerchief at the droplets that pearled from the stitch lines of his tent. He had wanted to be alone but being alone in a thunderstorm was not only alone but dangerous. He was glad the oak tree had fallen some time ago. Otherwise it might have taken him out. He'd heard of that happening. One moment you're here and the next you're dead and gone. Maybe in your sleep if you're lucky. He swirled the whiskey in his flask and took another swig. It was more than three-quarters gone. Three-quarters dead.

He heard something.

Lightning flashed and antlers imprinted themselves on his tent.

An angry roar.

The Goatman?

★★★★★

Daniel woke later that night and unzipped the tent fly. The storm had moved on. The moon was gibbous and the world silvery white with wet reflections. He wondered how he had ever fallen asleep with the storm tearing at his senses, the way it raised the banal to the claustrophobic, and the claustrophobic to the horrific.

The trees dripped. He imagined a mangled body dripping blood. He imagined hoofmarks.

There was a creature in the shadows. That's what had disturbed his sleep. The leaves of the underbrush trembled and the creature waddled out of stippled darkness into the brilliant moonlight. A possum. For a moment, Daniel retained the impression of the roadkill possum he had encountered earlier in his pilgrimage. He saw a bloated caricature of death, teeth jutted from a crushed skull, the hind legs dragging behind broken and useless. There was the stench of meat rot, the buzz of flies intent on flesh, on burrowing and procreation. But the vision passed and was replaced by the amiable beast he knew so well from his Madison neighborhood, its stench only that of garbage, of the cast-off ambrosia from local picnickers, its ghostly aspect just the glow of moonlit fur.

The possum waddled toward him. It snuffled and pawed at the leaf mulch. He thought it was headed in his direction but that was typical human ego, the placement of himself front and center of all behavior. The possum's path wavered, perhaps dictated by the scent of food, and it waddled off, still visible but following an erratic circle in the wet clearing.

Other creatures were also on the move. A raccoon and a squirrel crawled out from under the toppled oak. A deer poked its head from behind a branch and sniffed the air, a buck and Daniel's heart fluttered when he saw its antlers. A gargantuan toad hopped into view. A garter snake. Leaves rasped, wet as they were, with the scratch of chitinous legs. Crows and hawks haunted the branches and a barred owl demanded, "Who-cooks-for-you?" Daniel wanted them to hush but there was no way to cry out without calling attention to himself. His world was in motion, nothing stable, grunts and moans, whistles and shrieks, creatures of the forest and air congregating, rustling in the bracken, the dripping leaves.

He had almost become accustomed to this polyphonic intrusion when all went silent. He listened, trapped between exhalation and inhalation. The air in his lungs drained of sustenance and he needed to take another breath but was afraid. Just when he was about to give in to the dictates of his lungs burning from the lack of oxygen, there was a noise from above that had nothing to do with anything he'd heard before, a noise that sucked the remaining oxygen from his lungs and choked him like a boulder stuffed down his throat.

Announced by a flurry of wet leaves, of crumbled bark, the creature that interjected itself crawled headfirst down the trunk of a nearby oak like a giant but misshapen fly. Daniel had the impression of fur where the moonlight struck, but also glints that might have been wetness, or glittering shell, or eyes. Hardly had it come into view but the thing leaped. It crashed somewhere beyond the downed oak. There was then silence for a spell as the creature lurked just beyond the edge of perception, immobile except perhaps for the twitch of a nostril, the blink of an eye, as it devoured the scents and sights of the sopping forest and the waiting mob of creatures. Its silence had nothing

to do with fear and when it chose to move the saplings shivered and cried. Raindrops shaken loose from the branches pattered to the ground. Daniel listened, listened so hard that it seemed his entire life had been spent sitting within a petrified body and listening to the disturbing movements of that thing outside his field of vision.

Then, almost as an afterthought, the creature shoved its way into the moonlit clearing. Parts of its misshapen body snagged as it pushed through the branches and the ripped portions writhed with independent life. In its presence, the glamour fell from the animals outside Daniel's tent and he saw these for what they were—his fleeting earlier impression confirmed—the crushed and bloodied roadkill he had encountered on the highway. The forest floor pulsed with their resurrected corpses. Their dead muscles twitched as if galvanized by the earlier storm and a rippling carpet of torn and rotted flesh coalesced around and swarmed up the great creature's legs, becoming part of the creature as they did so.

The creature rose on its hind legs, so much taller than Daniel, still growing, its hairy antlered body looming against the purple sky, bulging and shifting and changing in form as new flesh and fur settled into place. The buck that had earlier thrust its head among the branches now crashed through and limped forward on splintered legs, stumbling on its own entrails. It leaped. It clawed its way to the creature's bristling summit to lay its head down in peace, antlers lost within a thicket of jagged bone that extended further into the forest canopy than Daniel could hope to see.

The creature bent forward. The eyes of its patchwork pelt glittered like stars. Daniel at last found voice and screamed the name of the one person who had been on his mind all that day, that long lonely month following her phone call on July fifth when she explained that their relationship was dead and gone, ashes of a fire that had burnt itself out: "Melody!"

★★★★★

In response to the dying shriek of a small animal, the goat-like creature apparates from a centuries-old wood. Below is a broke-down wagon with its virginal bride. The horses had swerved to avoid a rabbit, too late, and dragged the wagon into a ditch, one wheel splintering. The husband kicks the rabbit's corpse, curses it with all of Hell's fury for disturbing his wedding night, the bounty of his anticipated congress. He hikes back along the road for help but hardly has he passed beyond sight but the Goatman lopes down the hill. The Goatman bends over the roadkill rabbit and clutches the ruptured pieces to his breast. The newly acquired fur adheres in a ghostly cross. The Goatman then turns his attention to the wagon in which crouches the bride. She cannot hold her breath long enough to assume silence, nor hide the warmth of her body, nor her womanly scent. The creature circles. He sniffs at the wagon's cracks. A pink erection protrudes past the matted hair at his belly and the air is thick with musk. The Goatman bends over, erection still exposed, and whispers something to the space between the wagon slats. He whispers a secret to be shared only with his quarry. The young woman rises from hiding, fearless now, and descends from the wagon. She removes one shoe and then the other, throws these aside. The grassy marge is cool, ticklish against her naked feet. She giggles, laughs with the release that comes when fear and want are forgotten. The Goatman lays her gently on the grass and penetrates her with his long curved prick. The virgin bride cries out in a traitorous pleasure that means the end of her new husband, of all she once loved and of all she now renounces.

★★★★★

"Melody!"

Daniel woke to brilliant daylight, overheated by sun on the nylon tent skin. His cheeks burned, his body felt heavy as if weighted with warm earth, the air in the tent gelatinous, suffocating. He was naked. Jism had dried in itchy streaks across his belly and thighs. He scratched. He rose to a full sitting position and cried out in pain. A splitting headache as if the Goatman had plunged a claw or antler through his forehead. He struggled into his jeans and winced pulling on his dirty t-shirt.

The sod outside his tent was mashed and torn, the earth beneath the graffiti-etched cliff mutilated, scarred by claw, pad, and hoof prints. A sunbeam highlighted the sculpted Goatman and its eyes, dark beneath the protruding brow, watched over the remnants of the nighttime ceremony. There are portraits whose eyes seem to follow the observer but Daniel seemed beneath the image's notice, less real than its horrific original, than the nighttime assemblage of lost and maimed creatures of the highway.

Daniel furiously rubbed his face and sparks spangled the darkness behind his eyelids. He tried to convince himself the events of the previous night were nothing but whiskey-induced delirium, a subliminal haunting encouraged by the graffiti of local delinquents, but when he unburied his face everything was as before. He was the interloper and of less significance than the lingering scent of musk, than the weird tracks in the dirt. He traced the edge of a jagged hoofprint with his forefinger. If anything he was the memory here, the ghost out of time. He had to leave, and quickly.

He considered his tent, his weighty pack, and felt despair. Let someone else have it all. Unfreighted, he retraced his steps up the winding path through the woods to the Festge Park shelter. His body was so tired that his muscles seemed to contract and release without sensation. It was as if he were a puppet and his power of movement conferred by strings manipulated by a distant puppeteer although he, miraculously, was both puppet and puppeteer.

Families had already staked claims to the picnic tables in the park. "Excuse me," Daniel said as he sidestepped a woman, her arms encircling two bulging bags of groceries. She didn't notice her near miss and called out to her children, "Get away from that dirty grill and help me with the food."

There was a fresh crop of roadkill on route 14. Daniel now recognized these as integral to the highway and its tortured history. He thought of a mouse trod beneath a horse's iron-shod hoof, of a rabbit's back broken by a wagon wheel, and of the escalation wrought by Henry Ford and his potent dream of a car for the great multitude. What had we inadvertently birthed with our technologies and their callous horrors? What new form might an ancient god take when faced with an industrial revolution and the destruction of his wild realm?

There was a rustle and he turned to see the grass twitch by the blacktop. It was a robin, a wing broken but still attempting to fly, only to fail, and to fail again. It shivered in fear but it dared not cry. Its skull was bent, lop-sided. Daniel did the only thing that made sense. He searched out a boulder, carried it to where the bird struggled against its fate, and slammed it down on the creature's head. He felt the bird's death as a slight resistance but nothing more. He raised the stone and dropped it to the side. The bird was a crumpled mess of bloodied feathers but, come nightfall, it might live again.

The Goatman!

★★★★★

By the time Daniel reached Cross Plains, his thoughts fluttered with new possibilities in spite of his bone-weariness. Maybe he could set up a motion-activated camera to record the events at Festge Park. Maybe he would be lucky enough to actually document an apparition by the Goatman. Daniel imagined himself on the evening news, narrating an infrared video of the gruesome creature as it crawled down from the piney sky, as it rose from among the haunted dead and as it then subsumed them into its flesh. Daniel had seen enough horror movies to consider the possibility that the Goatman's image might not translate to video but, at the very least, he could identify the hooligans who caroused by their graffiti-scarred altar.

He felt a sudden searing pain in his forehead. He cricked his neck, knuckled a spot just above his eyebrows. The pain abated. When he opened his eyes, he discovered he faced the emerald hill where he had encountered Gerald the day before. Had it really been only a day? There might be no simple resolutions in life—Daniel still wasn't sure if his relationship with Melody was over or not, or where his research was headed—but one thing still rankled. The way Gerald had treated him. Gerald had acted as if Daniel was a nobody, a putz, just because he didn't live on the nosebleed heights above a fucking cornfield. Daniel couldn't, he shouldn't, let that rest. Besides he was almost sure, in spite of that disconcerting rumble of thunder, that Gerald's parting words to him had been, "Give my regards to the Goatman."

It was still the weekend and a chance meeting with Gerald was unlikely but not out of the question. If nothing else, Daniel could go knocking from door to door. He smiled thinking of the bland Gerald answering his knock, totally unsuspecting, his stunned confusion at the intrusion of a dirty stranger, and then the shock of recognition that this was no stranger but the same young man he had abused the day before.

"I'm not gotten rid of so easily," Daniel said, growling to himself as he hiked up the rutted trail beneath the powerline. He skirted a patch of poison ivy, the jagged whips of a blackberry bush. The feral hooks clawed at his jeans and he almost felt their penetration, the painful welling of blood. He winced and the world shuddered and righted itself. The blackberry bush was already behind him.

The trail was discolored a little ways down from where Daniel had eaten lunch. The dirt had a ruddy crust, in some places wan from the previous night's storm, in others flecked like rust where dried in the morning sun. Daniel felt an unhealthy constriction in his chest when he looked at that dark splotch, a strange taste in his mouth, like a bruise that would not heal. He licked his teeth, his gums. His forehead throbbed.

From off to his right, from within the depths of the forest, he heard song. Someone singing. He strained to make out the words. "Bar bar bar bar Barbar Ann."

He turned aside from the trail, moving stealthily, the wet underbrush deadening his footsteps. He followed a drag mark into the woods.

The singer's voice was familiar. "Barbara Ann. Bar bar bar bar Barbar Ann. You got me rockin' and a rollin', rockin' and a reelin' Barbara Ann."

It was Gerald. Daniel had planned for such a meeting, had half-expected it but still, now that he saw that dim shape hunched and dappled in the forest light, it was all he could do but to shout out in recognition.

"Tried Betty Sue. Tried Betty Lou. Tried Mary Sue, but I knew she wouldn't do. Bar bar bar bar Barbar Ann." Gerald had a shovel in his hands, the folding type that you store in a car trunk for emergencies. He dug at a mound of loose soil and leaf mulch.

Daniel edged closer, slipping from tree to tree and spying from the safety of their shadows. The rain-dampened leaves did not even whisper his presence.

Gerald pursed his lips for each syllable of that decades-old song. "Bar bar bar bar Barbar Ann. Bar bar bar bar Barbar Ann." His sleeves were rolled to the elbow and perspiration darkened the fabric at his armpits. There was a tattoo on his left forearm. It was surprisingly crude, like something done at home with a sewing needle dipped in the ink from a ballpoint pen. But there was a resemblance to the antlers on the leering devil on the Festge Park bluff.

Gerald's shovel grated against stone, sending a shiver down Daniel's spine. There were some boulders beneath the soil and leaves. Gerald set aside his shovel. He hauled the boulders from their resting places and piled them alongside the shallow trench he had excavated. It wasn't so much a trench as a grave. There was a body hidden beneath the forest debris: a bloodied skull with smeared hair, a dirty blue t-shirt, a twisted arm. The t-shirt looked familiar. Gerald stopped singing and arched his back, tired but luxuriating in his accomplishment. He tugged at the arm of the corpse and it shifted with an audible crack.

Daniel gritted his teeth in sympathetic pain. He had snuck closer during the exhumation. It was surprising that Gerald had not seen him, but he was engrossed in his efforts.

Gerald gave the recalcitrant arm another tug and the corpse shifted in its hollow such that the skull stared skyward. There before Daniel was the body, his body, his face. He stared. He refused for a moment to admit to what he saw. The face, his face, was ripped to shreds, dirt and gravel embedded in the flesh, bloodied and bruised, but there was no mistaking his own familiar features. There was a blood-smeared exit wound in the skull's forehead, and Daniel remembered the crack of thunder and Gerald's dismissive cry, "Give my regards to the Goatman."

"No!" Daniel screamed.

★★★★★

Gerald did not respond to Daniel's cry. Perhaps he cocked his head as if to hear a mumbled evocation, the rustle of wind through the damp leaves even though there was no wind, but that might have been Daniel's imagination.

Daniel rushed at his antagonist. For a moment it seemed they struggled—bodies collapsed together, the smell of sweat, deodorant; a chokehold, Gerald's unshaven chin digging into tensed muscle, Daniel's forearm constricting; a strangled cough; Gerald's knees collapsing as he tumbled into the grave—but then the air roiled, Daniel clutched for something that slipped away like dream fog, and he was face to face with the scabby trunk of a pine tree.

"Bar bar bar bar Barbar Ann. Bar bar bar bar Barbar Ann." Daniel whirled. Gerald stood beside the grave, merrily singing, head bouncing along to the beat. He was oblivious to Daniel's attack. He hadn't noticed, much less felt a thing.

The torn body in the grave was still Daniel's.

Daniel stared at his hands, pressed his palms together, felt resistance. Imagined resistance? He pushed and the fingers of each hand penetrated and then protruded from the back of the other like the wings of a malformed butterfly. He jerked his hands apart but it was too late to unsee that physical impossibility.

He was dead all right.

Nausea strangled his guts. He was just a spirit sleepwalking through a life he had already lost, making plans. The future no longer included him. It hurt to think about that. "Give my regards to the Goatman." The shock as the bullet penetrating his brain kindled within Daniel. He grimaced, remembered now his headfirst tumble down the powerline slope, his body slamming to earth, blood pooling beneath his skull. And then his walking on, disbelieving what had just happened, his body forgotten behind him.

Daniel ran a ghostly hand across his scalp. The hair at the back of his head was gummy and there was a hole beneath it, one just large enough for him to fit a finger into. The nausea returned and he stopped before he probed too deeply. There was another hole in his forehead, a crater. Bits of bone clung to tatters of exploded skin. There was mushy stuff inside the hole and the mushy stuff felt like loose scrambled eggs.

Gerald had buried Daniel's corpse but had now returned and partially exhumed it. Something was left undone. Flies had already settled on the caked blood, on the dried snot and tears. Daniel felt the tickle of their tiny legs, their sucking mouthparts at the gummy corners of his eyes.

Gerald swallowed a few times, Adam's apple bobbing, and spat on the bloodied face. Daniel shook his head in disgust, wiped but found nothing. Gerald pulled a pair of pruning sheers from his pants pocket and crouched beside the grave. He pushed the corpse's blood-clotted hair aside with the tip of the sheers. He did this gently as if administering rites. He then slid the sheers upward from the jaw to pinch Daniel's ear between the blades. He grasped the tip of the ear with his free hand.

He snipped.

Daniel screamed and clapped a hand to the side of his head. Blood spurted stickily between his fingers but, when he brought his hand to the fore, it was clean. His ear was gone, cut flush to the scalp, another hole in his already riddled skull.

Gerald unbuttoned the top button of his shirt. He pulled at a cord around his neck and withdrew a leather bag he had hidden against his chest. He cleaned the cut edge of Daniel's ear against some wet leaves and shoved it into the bag. There were other ears inside, other souvenirs. These were wrinkled like dried apricots.

Throughout this time, almost without realizing it, Daniel had edged closer to his grave. He peered over Gerald's shoulder. He smelled sweat and shampoo. He smelled deodorant. Hate pulsed within him and he flailed at Gerald's skull. His fist swooped through the air but there wasn't even the semblance of a landed blow. He had lost even that fictitious attachment to the world. All he had left was the broken body in the grave, his one true home.

The hole blasted by the bullet beckoned and Daniel crawled into his skull and curled up inside. There was plenty of room. There was also a strange comfort to being back in his body, broken as it was.

Slowly, methodically, Gerald refilled the grave.

Daniel watched as Gerald replaced the boulders, felt their suffocating weight on his chest, his arms, his face. Then the showers of dirt, sifting, dribbling through the cracks and puddling across his eyes. He tried to blink away the grit but could not. All he could do now was listen. Gerald gathered handfuls of leaves and scattered these across the surface of the grave, distributed these with the point of his shovel. Then there was the thrum of Gerald's footsteps receding. Then there was one last fading chorus of that hellish song, "Bar bar bar bar Barbar Ann. Bar bar bar bar Barbar Ann."

The forest's silence lasted for only a little while. Gradually, savoring their freedom from human incursion, squirrels began to chitter, sparrows tittered and crows cawed, branches scraped and sighed in the wind. The cacophony of the living drowned out the imprecations of the dead. Restlessly, Daniel waited for the release, the rejuvenation that might come with nightfall, with the dark rise of the Goatman.

★★★★★

"'You're killing me,'" Melody said. She was riding shotgun, Toby driving even though it was her Toyota. She'd had two glasses of wine and knew her limits.

"Really?"

"Honest to God, that's what he said." There was a barn dance that night in Cross Plains, a fund-raiser to eradicate the sumacs that displaced the native trees at Festge Park. They'd missed the potluck but Melody said she was more interested in dancing than in some stranger's questionable cooking.

"Is he always so melodramatic?"

"I told him off. You bet I told him off. No one talks to me like that."

"This happened a month ago?"

"On the fourth of July."

"But you still went to see the fireworks, right?"

Melody smiled but did not answer. She liked that Toby understood this about her.

Toby didn't see her smile. "Right?"

"Of course you're right." She relaxed. "You're also right that it was over a month ago." Her hand crept across the space that divided them and, with only minimal effort, she slipped her fingers into his jeans pocket. She began to play with his cock. It stiffened in response.

"Jesus!" Toby cranked hard on the steering wheel. The car swerved right, rocked, bumped across something. The rumble strip vibrated. The left set of wheels skated the asphalt marge, the other sprayed dirt.

"Jesus!" Toby repeated himself. He ducked at a shadow, but then regained control of the car and swung back across the rumble strip, still in his lane. He gulped for air. His arms shivered with adrenalin but he did not slow. He did not want to slow down.

"What was that?"

"There was something on the road."

"An animal?

"A deer, probably. It was hard to make out." He tried to smile. "I was distracted." Toby didn't tell Melody that the body looked nothing like any deer he'd ever seen. He tried not to look in the rearview mirror but failed, barely aware of Melody's questions.

Behind him, the thing he'd run over struggled to rise. It fell several times, its leg collapsing at a broken angle. It crawled. It dragged itself across the remaining strip of asphalt, the rumble strip. It tumbled into the ditch beside the road, still crawling. Other dim broken shapes joined it from the shadows and then everything was shadow, everything was night and disappearing behind Toby as he pressed down on the accelerator.

"Do you want to go back and check?"

"No." Toby tried to hold his voice steady, to block out that last imperfect vision. "It was dead, whatever it was." ▪

THE EVER-PRESENT AND ENDURING LIST

[Joseph F. Nacino]

Somewhere in the hot, humid city of Metro Manila, a young man in black sat before a ramshackle eatery located in the middle of a small alleyway. Though it was already nearing midnight, the summer heat had only slightly abated when the sun went down. The air felt sticky, and sweat ran freely underneath his ragged *Killjoys* t-shirt.

As the small grandmother manning the eatery cooked a pot of the blood dish dinuguan, the young man's head blissfully nodded along to Assembly General's "Kontrabida" music video playing on his phone, the music slightly audible despite his earphones.

Just then, an ad interrupted the YouTube video, showing the President standing at the podium and preparing to speak.

"*Ay putragis!*" Oskar swore.

The ad was about the midnight presidential press conferences, the President swearing and rambling again about killing all monsters. In one hand, the President held a tablet and was gesticulating with it. The much-vaunted *List*, Oskar thought, the one that supposedly bore the names of thousands and thousands of monsters, half-breeds and quarter-bloods, and even the lords and ladies of the fey *diwata* living in the country.

Oskar shook his head. Right now, the President's midnight messages were everywhere: aside from being telecast simultaneously on TV and radio, the government's telecoms agency also bought space in YouTube, Google, and Facebook. Likewise, the electronic billboards throughout the metro showed the midnight presscon as well as the names on the *List*.

You also couldn't escape the *List*. It was what everyone was talking about—and feared. Nobody knew how the government compiled their *List*. Some people figured that the police and community officials were required to submit a quota of names every month. Others warned that those who criticized the government would be added to the *List*, given that several well-known critics had already been arrested.

But that was the problem of the *List*. No one really knew who was an *aswang* or a *dwende* or a *diwata*. After hiding in myths and legends for decades, they had come down from the high mountains and the dark forests to immerse themselves in the local population with their enchantments and shape-shifting powers. A lot of them even had gotten jobs and married humans to have half-breed and quarter-blood children.

Unfortunately, a lot of accusations of who were monsters and who were not were just based on suspicions and old grudges, leading to attacks by supporters of the President, the police, and people who realized that they could finally get their payback against those who owe them.

Sighing, Oskar figured it was time to go to work. Waving goodbye to the grandmother—who gave a toothy grin back as she stirred the pot of *dinuguan*—Oskar walked towards one of the massive trees that lined Balete Street. As he exited the alleyway, a trio of policemen bearing high-powered firearms and wearing balaclava masks to hide their faces passed him by. Stepping to one side, he made himself as quiet and unnoticeable as possible. You never knew if the police would suddenly get into their heads that he was a suspected monster.

Once they were gone, he took off his earphones and sidled up to the tree. There were two reasons why he always ate at the eatery regularly: the always-fresh *dinuguan* and the nearby *balete* trees. As he stood under the wide branches of the tree, he called up, "Hey, Berto! Let's go!"

One of the shadows moved away from the tree, revealing itself to be a *tikbalang*: a tall, muscular creature with a horse's head, and stood upright on a pair of horse-shaped legs. Berto gave a snort and said, "Where have you been? I've been waiting for hours."

"I thought we were supposed to meet at midnight!" Oskar said in exasperation.

"That's not what Marlon told me!"

Oskar sighed. "You should always be careful with what a *thalon* tells you, you know."

Berto snorted again. "I'll tie Marlon's four feet together and throw him into the Pasig River, that's what I'll do next time I see him."

"Never mind. It's time to head out."

As Berto half-knelt on the ground, Oskar jumped onto his back. With one hand, he put on one of his earphones. He asked: "You have your earpiece on?"

The *tikbalang* stood up and tapped one ear. "Yup."

"All right," Oskar said. "Let's go."

Berto started running, first a slow jog as he got used to Oskar's weight, and then he started going faster. Soon, everything around them was a blur as the *tikbalang* sped through the streets of Sta. Mesa, running faster than any normal human or horse.

Oskar figured they would have been a strange sight to see: a man clinging to the back of a running half-human, half-horse creature. However, he knew that Berto's enchantments were at work, such that people would only see a helmeted man on a speeding motorcycle.

His phone suddenly chirped as a call came in. He said: "Hello, Leah? Talk to me."

Oskar tried to imagine Leah flying high above them: the *manananggal's* shadowy half-torso unseen against the dark clouds, bat wings flapping occasionally, and viscera trailing from the upper half of her body.

"A hit team just left the police substation," Leah replied, her voice barely audible against the night wind. "I think this is the one."

Oskar asked. "Where is it going?"

"It's heading for Tondo," she said, "I think that's Elias and his family."

"That's the *Santelmo*. Not a good idea if he starts burning things with shanty houses built so close," he said. "Who's in that area who can help?"

Berto answered for her, turning his head so that Oskar could hear him: "That's Ramon and Marlon. And Mang Bong is ready to provide an exit."

Oskar squeezed Berto's shoulder in acknowledgement and spoke on his phone: "Thanks Leah. Keep an eye out for any other teams out there. We're headed over to Tondo."

"Be careful!"

"We will," Oskar replied before he hung up on the call. Next, he rang up the *thalon*. "Marlon, get your ass ready. The hit team is on its way there."

"Oh, so I guess the people I'm following now are just dressed in black clothes and masks for kicks?"

Oskar swore under his breath. He said, "Shut up and listen to me, Marlon. Distract them, but don't get caught. They're targeting Elias and his family. Berto and I will try to get to Elias' place as fast as we can to pull them out."

"Consider them distracted," Marlon said, and hung up. Even through the phone, Oskar heard the smug tone in Marlon's voice. But he tried not to worry. As it was, *thalons* were too weird to be seen on the streets: they looked like regular dogs except for their backward-facing human feet and human faces.

What did worry him was that *thalons* were also known to be tricksters, constantly shadowing humans invisibly. He wouldn't put it past Marlon to play a prank on the hit team that would bite the *thalon* back in the ass.

He managed to call Ramon and Mang Bong, and got them to meet them at Elias' place. But the two were just there to help: it was up to him and Berto to rescue Elias and his family.

"You know where Elias lives, right?" Oskar asked.

"Yup," Berto said as he turned into Roxas Boulevard. "We'll get there fast, or I'm not a *tikbalang*."

In a few moments, they had passed the North Harbor port but Berto jumped over the sidewalk to take the side streets. "This is faster," he said as he ran from one *eskinita* into another.

Just then, a small dog with a wagging tail and a human face appeared before them in the middle of the alleyway. Berto skidded to a halt.

"What took you so long?" it said as it licked a bleeding flank.

Oskar jumped down from the tikbalang's back and cried, "Dammit, Marlon, I told you not to get too close to them."

The *thalon* shook its head: "Pffft. Just a scratch. I managed to get half of them lost among the maze of houses when one of them decided to take potshots at me out of frustration."

Berto shook his head, his mane flying like a flag. He put a massive hand on Marlon's black furry head: "Stupid. You're going to get yourself killed one of these days."

The *thalon* laughed before replying: "They have to catch me first, Berto."

Oskar waved at Berto. "C'mon, we need to get to Elias' house.

Go have that looked at, Marlon."

Marlon gave them a dog's grin and then loped off into the darkness.

It was a short run to their destination, through the *eskinitas* that served as the highways and byways for the poor people living in the mass of ramshackle houses. Even with the lateness of the hour, it was strange to see no one on the streets, given that Tondo was one of the most populous—and poorest—districts in the city of Manila. Oskar remembered a time when this area would full of people just hanging around and drinking local gin on makeshift benches.

Though Berto could have gotten there faster than Oskar, the *tikbalang* hung back to keep pace with him. That was why they were able to spot the first spotter near Elias' house.

Hiding behind a low stone wall, Oskar pointed at the masked policeman bearing an assault rifle standing at the entrance to an alleyway. Berto, barely hidden underneath a stunted *yakal* tree, nodded silently. Just as the spotter looked away, the *tikbalang* dashed forward. In a blink of an eye, the policeman was down on the ground with a broken neck courtesy of Berto's giant hands.

The two ran into the alleyway. There were no lights in this area: the police had broken the few lightbulbs residents had installed. Oskar pointed at the glass fragments on the ground that would make anyone hear of their approach.

Far ahead, they saw a sole light coming from the door of a house. They also heard shouts of "Don't come out!" and "Stay inside if you know what's good for you!"

Oskar grimaced. Hit teams had the habit of threatening nearby civilians so that there wouldn't be any witnesses. But even with if there were, the hit teams usually acted with impunity anyway.

"Those bastards!" Berto growled and whispered. "I'll take out the ones outside! You go inside!"

As the *tikbalang* dashed forward, Oskar speed dialed Leah's phone and said: "Leah, can you help Berto?"

"I'm on it!"

As Oskar ran towards the house, he saw the *tikbalang* zigzag towards the two policemen guarding the other end of the alleyway. One policeman saw Berto and raised his M4 carbine to fire, and his partner did the same without a second thought.

They both missed, giving Berto a chance to kick one policeman in the chest. That policeman slammed against the far wall of a house and slid to the floor coughing blood. The other dropped his rifle and tried to draw his pistol, but Berto grabbed his tactical vest with one hand. The tikbalang then started pounding on the man's face.

There was the beat of wings above Oskar and he looked up to see a third policeman struggling as he was dragged upward by Leah, her pretty doll-like face visible against the night sky. Oskar hoped she wasn't hungry.

He ran to the house and peered into a window. He saw the reason for the bright light: Elias was slowly transforming from his human shape into a giant glowing ball of fire.

"Stay back!" Elias shouted in defiance as he confronted the two policemen who were aiming their guns at him. "Don't hurt my family!"

Behind Elias was his family. Oskar recognized Elias' wife, Marian, and their two kids, Alyssa and Joy. All of them were crying in fear.

Scowling, Oskar stepped into the house. He grabbed both policemen from the back of their tactical vests and easily hauled them outside the house. He shouted to the family: "Stay here!"

A policeman in each hand, Oskar threw both against a pile of garbage. Shaken and surprised, the two were still able to fire their guns at Oskar. Most of the bullets missed but one hit him on the side of the head, snapping him back though he still managed to keep his footing.

An aghast policeman stared at Oskar standing over them, his head hanging over his back attached to just a flap of skin. "My God! What are you!?" he said.

Oskar laughed, a deep and grating sound as if a thousand sharp teeth were gnashing. He lowered his torso so that the policemen could see the giant mouth where his head had been. "I guess your mothers never told you about the *Pugot Mamu* when you were children?"

Oskar smiled—and the policemen saw all his teeth—before he attacked. The men screamed.

Afterward, Oskar stepped back inside the house. Elias was back in his human form, holding the hands of his wife while their children clustered around them. Oskar wasn't sure who was comforting who.

"Are… are they gone?" Marian asked.

Oskar shrugged and said, "They're not a problem anymore. Is anyone hurt?"

Elias shook his head and said, "We're fine, just shook up. Thank you, Oskar. You came just in time."

"It's all good," Oskar replied. "You can't stay here though. More police will be coming soon."

"Where would we go?" Marian asked.

"We'll hide you," Oskar said with a gentle smile, before turning around and exiting the house. A fat man in jeans and a Fidel Castro shirt, as well as a dwarfish old man looking grumpy stood outside waiting for him.

"Where's Berto?" he said.

"He's moving around. Hard to hide without a tree around, he said," the fat man, Ramon, replied. The *busaw's* stomach was terribly distended. Oskar looked around and saw the bodies of the police were gone. However, there were several pieces of banana tree logs lying on the ground.

"I see you've disposed of the bodies," Oskar said. *Busaws* had the habit of replacing dead bodies with tree logs via magic. Like their ghoulish cousins the *bal-bal*, the *busaws* were carrion and fed on the dead.

"Of course," Ramon said, with a hint of a snake-like tongue peeking from behind his grin. "Just doing my part for the monster revolution."

"I told you a hundred times, there's no monster revolution," he replied in a tired tone. "There's only us."

"Well, who else is going to power the revolution?"

Oskar snorted and turned to the old man. "Can you bring Elias and his family out of here, Mang Bong?"

The nuno sa punso nodded and said, "Not much soil here but I'll do what I can."

Mang Bong skittered around to peer at the ground and finally found a patch that wasn't concrete. He drew a symbol on it and a small mound of soil drove itself up from the earth.

Oskar leaned inside the house and waved at Elias and his family. "Time to go," he said. "Follow Mang Bong. He'll know where to take you."

As they passed by, Elias shook his hand while Marian gave him a peck on the check. Oskar watched them follow the *nuno sa punso* down into a tunnel in the ground with Ramon waddling close behind them. Once they were gone, the mound collapsed into itself.

"Time to go?" said a deep voice behind him.

Oskar turned to see Berto standing watch in the shadows.

"Yes," he replied. "Still a lot of work to do tonight. A lot of our kind's names still on that list."

"We can't save them all, you know," Berto said as he kneeled down to let Oskar climb on his back.

"I know," he said. "But every one that we do save is worth it." ∎

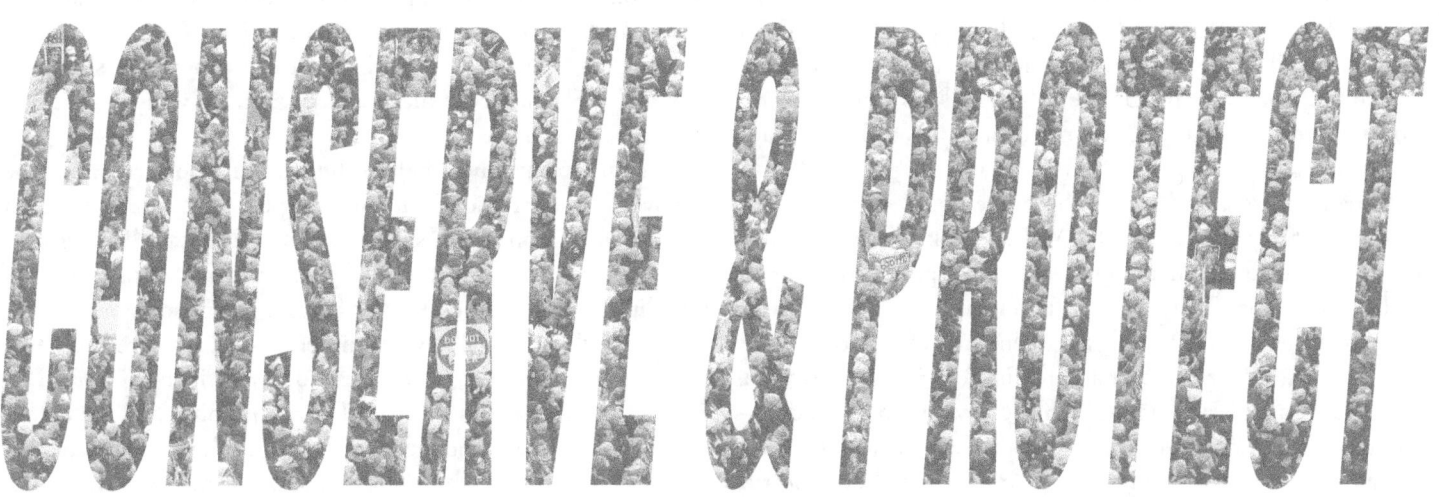

BEYOND THE MEATWALL OF FACTS

[Alex S. Johnson]

President Elect Maynard Shtroumph was having trouble with his tie.

It was a big, big tie, maybe the biggest ever worn by the Chief Executive. The problem was, it was too long.

Way, way too long.

He strongly suspected his uber-big-enemy CROOKED PILLORY had something to do with this. Big-time. Pillory was maybe the worst politician ever in the history of the universe. And that wasn't the fake news. That was direct from the source—God. He'd confirmed God's word from the deity's second in command, Louche Ramble.

Shtroumph observed that the tie—a big, bold, red PUSSY-GRABBER of a tie—seemed to be leering at him. The solid red of it had broken up the way his satellite feed from the real (non-fake) news sometimes did. The patterns it made now, jagged fragments of a face, a smile, the smile of a serpent, suggested interference from aliens. He considered an executive order forcing PILLORY to reveal her constituency. Those three million illegal voters from outer space should be held responsible for their theft of his legitimate win, not just in the electoral college, but the popular vote as well. He would make America first and the unpopular aliens even more unpopular than they already were. He picked up the phone.

"Muller, I want you to draft me an order. We need to send a message to the aliens that they cannot hack the solid red tie of the President of the…hello?"

The tie had slipped from his collar and hiked its way up to his neck. Shtroumph felt the familiar signs of strangulation—the increased heartbeat, the rise of his epic four inches (maybe the largest cock known to creation science), the surge in his balls. He found it hard to concentrate on Muller's babbling, especially now that his vision swam with thousands of globes all reflecting PILLORY's head. The serpent-lady from outer space needed a grabbing, one she sure as hell wasn't getting from that shit-eating grin of a failed ex-President, SHILL HINTON. But the current President's hands were already occupied. Where there was a will, there was a way to choke back with a vengeance. Shtroumph loosened his belt and fastened his fingers on the monster pressing its purple dome through his red, white and blue boxers.

Shtroumph glanced up at the office walls, the very, very important, bigly bad-ass walls. Andrew Jackson and Thomas Jefferson looked down at him with an approval rating that couldn't be beat. They got it. If anybody ever recognized his achievements—the only achievements of their kind an American President had ever accomplished—it was these icons of Roman Law. If Jackson and Jefferson were around today— and who said they weren't, along with that asset to his race, Douglass—they would have something to say about the tie-

hack. And they wouldn't block him from doing battle with his cock, forcing it to yield a righteous payload.

Distracted by an enormous swelling of pride and rod of steel, he placed the phone back in its mellow gold cradle and reached for the omni-remote. This would seal him inside the oval office and ensure his safety from all enemies furry and domesticated. By this time the tie had wound itself trebly around his neck and his eyes were bulging, more bulge than any eyes had shown since the short but vital reign of Emperor Bilgewater III in 1856. The liars said he couldn't read, but he was pretty sure he'd seen a reference to Emperor Bilgewater in a brief.

Or was that "in briefs?" He was pondering this and other significant questions when the phone rang. He took it on the fifth ring, making sure to admire his shifting Technicolor shades that crawled across his face as the tie did its work. He knew the American people applauded the rich carotene hue that covered every square inch of his svelte, sculpted body, but they deserved a wider choice. A choice he would give them as soon as that Jew Muller left him alone. Cannon had warned him never to fully trust a Hebe.

"Yes, this is the President."

"Sir, I've drafted that executive order. The National Guard has been put on full alert. Our borders must be protected from the aliens. Those politically correct bastards have a lot to answer for. If not now, when?"

"Agreed, Muller. I can't tell you how glad I am that I hired you. Is that it?"

"I'm sorry?"

"I said YOU'RE FIRED, Krassner. VERY, VERY NOT EMPLOYED BY ME. AND EXTREMELY VETTED. Cannon told me you support the two state solution, or the one state…I don't have time to investigate myself. I am the President of these United States. Many, many important responsibilities."

Shtroumph glanced at the portraits of Jackson and Jefferson, who had unzipped and held impressive sausage in their hands, slick with the original oil paint. Not as impressive as his own, but very, very big for their times. He slammed down the phone. If Muller called again, he was unavailable. And that was final.

He sank to his knees before the altar his good friends in the Alt Reich had provided for him—a platform draped with an American flag, on which stood a skull said to have been ripped directly from the head of Jihad Joe, brain still intact; a cross pre-dipped in gasoline for easy flaming purposes, and a scale-model patch of illegal lawn complete with the rusted remains of a car transmission on cinder blocks, all in miniature. His hands flowed over his thick shaft, and he could feel the cream as it bubbled from the glans, rich, full dollops of it. The red of his blood. The blue as the red showed through the white skin. And the white, ultra-mega-white SPERM…there would be tweeting after.

The phone tried to ring again but only managed to buzz and foam.

But something was wrong with the walls.

And this, more than anything else, concerned him. It concerned him more than he'd ever been concerned, which was big-time. It occupied his mind more bigly than his daughter's ass at his hottest, and wow, had Svetlana's ass achieved a hotness unsurpassed by history's parade of butt. His attention was torn between the walls, his approaching climax, the phone's odd silence, and other vital matters.

He'd wondered for a while now why the promised "wall of meat" his supporters had offered against the raving mad hordes of bad news bearers hadn't shown up. Ever. And why it was suddenly ripping the marble from the ovulating office's interior, stripping it down to a writhing, salmon-pink swatch of flesh. IF this wasn't just another show of alien force.

He watched as the Wall of Meat spread to every corner. He found it hard to breath now. He realized the tie had its serpent tongue buried in his neck. Injecting him with some kind of awful outer space venom. Which is when the heads began to pop from the meat.

Shtroumph's cock collapsed quick as a controlled demolition leveled a skyrise hotel in the center of Manhattan. Those heads—millions of them, brown and black ones, oh God, and some wearing JibJabs—were thrusting through the awful wall like mushrooms. And they were howling, howling for rights he, Shtroumph, had denied them. It was bad. It was worse than bad—it might be the single worst nightmare any living President had experienced while still awake. Biglier than Hinton's bad dreams within bad dreams, which he and Bullcrap had discussed over the nine hole course, that one fatal day.

He tried to tell them to SHUT UP. He screamed that they were all VERY FUCKING FIRED. He called the demons by their real names—VERY

FAKE. He threatened the nuclear option. HE WOULD KILL THEM ALL WITH FIRE. But all this did was rouse more heads to the surface.

Shtroumph scrambled to his feet, grasped the phone and prepared to dial, but it slipped from his sticky fingers and fell to the marble tile. Hands—millions of them, some brandishing kebabs—thrust up through the floor and grabbed at his shiny black Florsheim shoes. From the MEATWALL the heads yawned—quadrupillions of nasty facts, with row upon row of sharp, pointy teeth, and tongues like the PILLORY-HACKED TIE which had wriggled down his pants now and had his cock in its jaws—the worst, the most terrible biting—ever—in—the history of—the Presidency, stretched between alien heads gnawing and nibbling and gnashing and biting, tearing his hairpiece, digesting it, making great big holes in his face—the humanity—and the factual hands striped with a bazoollion colors, fastened around his ankles, pulling him down, down, down…stretched like taffy through and beyond a living, breathing meatwall of facts. ◼

DUMP THE CHUMP!

OR, AS IT'S AFFECTIONATELY KNOWN: THE NEXT GREAT ROCK N' ROLL SWINDLE

[John Palisano]

"Punk rock doesn't even exist anymore," Nick said, suspiciously eyeing the kid's iPhone, which was pointed at his head. He was convinced Hairy Barry was videoing him, too, despite his insistence he not. "It was a movement in the mid 70s that came and went faster than it could be co-opted by the mainstream."

Hairy Barry winced. "But Diz is real punk rock. Hard core. You guys are always ready to call people out on their shit."

Nick raised a finger. "Don't forget the women," he said. "We're not just a sausage fest."

"I know," Hairy Barry said. "It's just a matter of speech. It just fell out." He looked downward.

"Don't do that!" Nick scolded. "Every god damned word means something. Especially when you're recording. You need to learn that stat."

"Point taken. I will watch it. I didn't mean any . . .'"

"Of course you didn't. Fascists never do." Nick had turned away. He'd gotten his act down. Even the press folks he liked, he did his best to turn on at the end of the talk. It was expected of him. They were over there and we are over here. That's that. Don't intermingle. They will sell you out to the highest bidder without a second thought. Just business. They always said that. Just another opportunist fucking capitalist.

And hell of hells, he needed another coffee.

★ ★ ★ ★ ★

"Did you refer to your interviewer as Hairy Barry?" Katie raised her guitar at Nick, pointing the headstock at his head as though it were a gun.

Nick pulled at his bare chin. "He had one of those beards that make him look like a lumberjack," he said. "I couldn't help it. Very distracting."

"He writes for USA Today," Katie said.

"Ah, hell," Nick said. "That guy? Really?"

"Really," she said.

He wrapped his hands around his mic stand. "Well if you tossers would actually do interviews once in awhile, maybe I wouldn't have to. I hate all this micro-management of our image and stuff. Have we turned into KISS or something here?"

"You're the voice of the band," Iko said, looking down at her sea foam green Fender telecaster, strumming it absently. "Always have been, always will be."

"Well then lay off," Nick said. "Everyone knows I'm awful."

"Especially us," Katie said, giving him the finger.

He gave it right back. "Love you, too, sunshine."

The soundcheck roared to life as the first tom hits of "Weird and Wonderful" echoed through the empty Borders Arena—a brand that'd been resurrected from the dead, just like: "The band that wouldn't die."

Behind them hung the new backdrop. The artwork portrayed a pseudo-spray painted logo of their name—Diz—short for Diz Topia. The full name had been dropped years earlier, shortened with their nickname. Everyone knew which band it was, anyway. "We're like Van Halen meets the Dead Boys," Nick had often said, "only nowhere near as fun."

Nick looked around at his bandmates and laughed. *Look at us idiots still standing up here, selling out these big places. Such a long way from that stupid van that always broke down.*

His mood broke.

"Wait! Wait! Wait!" The last one was screamed full force. "What the hell is that?" He pointed at the opposite side of the arena.

Two huge vinyl posters hung, presidential nominee Rick Ross portrayed as a stylized cartoon, his awful slogan in huge, classic Russian propaganda font: ROSS THE BOSS! THE RIGHT BOSS! THE RIGHT TIME!

Katie echoed. "Who said that's okay?"

"They've got the arena booked a few days next week," said their war weary road manager, Steve, over the PA's talkback.

"I don't give a dead man's balls," Katie said. "Get them down or we don't play."

★ ★ ★ ★ ★

Nick put down the remote control and rubbed his eyes. "I cannot believe you made me watch *Gilmore Girls* all night long," he said. "At least the mom is really hot."

Becka rubbed his arm. "But I'm worth the sacrifice, aren't I?"

"Sure," he said. "Of course."

"And you didn't even check your phone once," she said. "I think you know what that means. Reward time."

"Awesome," he said, and rolled over to kiss her. They did, for a moment, before she stopped him.

"I think we should both hit the bathroom first," she said. "You first."

Nick went.

A moment in, he heard his iPhone go off––a sound like twenty car alarms .

"Babe," he heard Becka call. "I thought you turned that thing off?"

He hollered back, "It is. That's the Red Phone mode."

"What?" she asked, not having heard him over the noise.

He hurried back and grabbed the phone. He pressed the big red graphic at the middle of the screen. "It's got Red Phone mode on it," he said. "If someone who has that calls, it overrides everything. Even if it is turned all the way off."

He swiped and saw the message. He kept reading it, again and again. "Rick Ross wants us to play his big party next week. A million dollars. Shit."

When he looked up at Becka, she smiled and pointed at his iPhone. "You're going to have to add me to that."

★ ★ ★ ★ ★

"We can't do it," Katie said. "Diz does not support candidates or politicians. We're against that. That's every damned thing we're not about rolled up in one bullshit filled burrito. Extra cheese."

Nick paced his apartment, looking over to Becka, who was focused on her own phone. "We can and we should," he said. "We can use the platform to make a statement. We can burn the house down."

"You idiot," Katie said. "Didn't you read the demands?"

"Demands?"

"Yeah. Did you even bother to scroll down the message, just a little bit, you knuckledragger?"

He knew he was caught. "What'd I miss?"

"There's explicit terms not to say anything bad about Ross from the stage or throughout the campaign," she said.

"Shit." In his mind, he'd already spent his portion of the money. The epic month-long vacation with Becka in South France was off, god damn it all to hell.

"They're even telling us what songs are okay and not okay," Katie said. "It's a bad deal."

He spilled out every curse word he know, both real and made up. "There's got to be a way."

★ ★ ★ ★ ★

Dear Nicky Diz, Katie, Iko and Charlie (best hair in rock n' roll!),

I just wanted to reach out and tell you I was mortified to see the clip on YouTube of you getting upset my posters were still up during your soundcheck at the New Borders Arena. It broke my heart, as I grew up with the band, and have always thought, had I the chance, I'd make you proud of the generation you inspired. My path to politics was forged on being fair and even and not the typical mudslinging and horrors we've come to know.

To make it up to you, I'd like to offer the band a million dollars to perform at my election rally at the end of October. I'd pay the money up front, and it would come to you personally, from me, instead of campaign funds. The truth is right there, in the middle, plain as day. A million bucks. Play my rally. Everyone's happy.

Thanks for the inspiration,
Rick Ross
"The Right Boss! The Right Time!"

★ ★ ★ ★ ★

"I don't believe a word he says," Nick said. "He's good. I'll give him that. Knows what to say. And on paper, I want to believe him. But I just have these awful dreams about him. Day dreams. There's something 'off' about the guy I just can't put my finger on."

"Right," Charlie said. Rick could hear him practicing his sticks on a couch while he talked.

"Jesus, man, can you stop that for five minutes?" Nick said. "Do you do anything other than drums and get your hair cut?"

"What else is there?" Charlie said.

"Lots, man. Lots. I just want to know where you stand on this."

"I'll support whatever the band wants to do." He'd stopped using both sticks, but Nick could hear he was still gently tapping a single stick.

"Charlie? You're in the band."

"I know. I know," he said. "It's just that I hate these political things. I guess, if a gun's to my head . . ."

"It is."

"Then I'd have to say let's do it. We can always give the money to the ACLU or something."

"You can give your part away," Rick said. He laughed.

"All right. Then it's settled."

★ ★ ★ ★ ★

Nick put pen to paper. He grabbed his trusted black telecaster and plugged it into his VOX amp. He didn't play guitar onstage anymore, but he still did so almost every day. Most of the time, he just riffed aimlessly while the TV was on, or played punk up versions of non-punk songs, but that day he had a melody spinning around his head like a flu germ sneezed in his face. It'd start small, but soon enough, it'd multiply until it infected his whole body and made him crazy.

"Dah-dah-dump. Dah-dah-dump. This guy's a chump. I don't care what he say." He stayed rooted on a G power chord, all downstrokes, while he worked out the song.

"Dump. Gump. Pump. Lump. Bump. What the heck rhymes with chump?" He kept at it. As soon as he stopped thinking, it rolled out of him in less than fifteen minutes.

★ ★ ★ ★ ★

Uncle Al Carmichael looked at the contract several times, turning it over. "I've been your attorney since the beginning," he said. "I'm not going to lie to you. This is a very oppressive contract, as far as what you can and can't do."

"Understood," Nick said. He shut his eyes and asked, "I am just wondering what they can do if we play and don't listen to them. Off the record. Confidentially."

"You wouldn't?"

Nick didn't say anything.

"What are you up to?"

"I just want to know if we could lose the money or if they could sue us or anything."

"They could, but without any specific penalizing clauses, it'd be hard for them to win a case. It says the few songs that are cleared, and lists a bunch that aren't."

"What about songs that aren't listed?"

"They've listed everything on your albums, as far as I can see."

"Let's say, hypothetically, there's a new one."

Uncle Al thought about it for a moment. Pulled on his dreads. "I suppose that would not be covered in the contract. Only that you'd have to perform two or three songs from the approved list."

"How much of a song is considered playing the song? The whole thing?"

"Well, the RIAA counts any recognizable portion of a song as a needle drop, and is required to be cleared and paid for, or stiff fines can result. The case of Dim Shores Records vs Martin Enterprises sealed that deal for us."

"So likely the reverse would hold up," he said. "Let's say we play a minute of a song. That would likely count."

"Likely."

"Okay, then," Nick said, a smug smile stretching across his bony face. "Tell them to send it in cash. Small bills."

★★★★★

"There's no way we can play this song," Katie looked upset. "It's great, but we'll have the Secret Service taking off their fake plastic hands and shooting us dead right up on stage. Or soon thereafter. I don't want any part of it."

"Don't be ridiculous," Nick said. "They can't do that. This is America. We have rights."

"Yeah. All three of them," Katie said.

"Come on. Seriously."

"I am being serious. It's not a good idea at all."

"I'll take the heat."

"You?"

"Tell everyone it was my idea. We can start 'Somewhere In Between' and then I will start 'Dump the Chump' and we will make it look like you're all just following along and didn't expect it."

"Risky," she said.

"Indeed."

"We don't even have time to properly learn it," Iko said. Everyone looked to her.

"Then it'll be perfect," Nick said. "And it's going to be about as real as it gets."

★★★★★

Nick looked out at the assembled crowd. There they were, back in the same arena they'd played less than a week earlier, but standing on someone else's stage, and about to perform in front of someone else's crowd. He clutched his black Telecaster. It'd be the first time he'd play it onstage since…well…he wasn't sure. It felt like a shield and an axe at the same time. If anyone got out of line, he'd have something to hit them with. If the Secret

Service opened fire, maybe they'd hit the guitar instead of on of his vitals.

Seven rows back, in a squared off section, he saw Rick Ross shaking hands and smiling. He looked like a damn movie star with his just-right salt and pepper hair and chiseled face. Nick thought for a moment about what it would have been like to grow up as him. What was his childhood like? His teen years? What made him turn out that way? What made him tick now? It was the same thing he secretly went through at every show. He'd pick one person, and throughout the night, focus on them and imagine their life from birth up until that moment. It made him connect to the audience. He sang his songs through them.

When he looked at Rick Ross he did not imagine his past, only his future. Nick saw people crying in the streets, holding themselves, bloody. He saw people wounded outside grocery stores. He saw children running alone, looking for their parents. Behind all of them, he saw troops. He heard gunfire. He heard screams until he heard silence. The scene played out in a blink in his mind as he stood in that moment, waiting for their cue. It was the nightmare he'd had a hundred times already. It burned inside his head like a dark, evil tapeworm, threatening to eat and take over his brain.

Rick Ross was bad. He didn't seem so, but he was. "A trojan horse from hell," he'd said to Becka. She'd agreed. The country would be lost as they'd known it under him. Rights would slowly get rolled back, and once that happened, the coup would roll in, the place would be ripe for their cleansing binge.

A comic from a Netflix show strode to the microphone at a podium stage left. As he spoke, Nick looked at his bandmates. No one made eye contact. It'd been a rough week. The fans were outraged. How could they? How could the band that stood for all things rebellion be playing a political rally? They felt betrayed. They felt angry. They felt pissed beyond pissed.

Nick knew. In a few minutes, the fans would know why.

The comic was done blathering.

Nick looked real quick at everyone. Charlie made eye contact, nodded, and started the beat to "Somewhere In Between".

Nick thought, Here we go, god damn it. Here we go."

They made it through the opening and the first verse.

> There's a guy on TV
> He's looking at you
> He's looking through me
> I ain't buyin' a word he says
>
> The Truth is Somewhere In Between
> Lies and promises always spinning
> Not today! No More!

He looked out and saw the suits dancing and trying to pogo, laughing at one another the same way housewives laugh when they think they're funny trying to cop some ghetto slam or pseudo-twerk.

Nick stopped singing and went to his G power chord. Rooted on it for a while.

Then he sang the new song looking right at Rick Ross.

Dump the Chump!
He'll bring the end to you and me
Something worse than anarchy
A brand new fascist regime
Taking place behind the scenes

Dump!
That! (pointing at Ross)
Chump!

As if on cue, the band nearly fell apart. They didn't know the changes. They didn't know the words. They looked lost. But they kept on.

The crowd wasn't dancing.

Rick Ross looked coldly at them. Someone said something into his ear and he nodded.

Dump the Chump!
It's worse than the same
His smile lies, his eyes betray
He's going to line us up
And blow us all away

Dump!
That!
Chump!

The new boss
Is worse than Mussolini
The new boss
Is into ethnic cleansing
The new boss
Will stab us while he's smiling

Secret Service had already rushed the stage. They made gestures to the sound and video crews to cut the power. It only took a few moments for them to do so.

Nick unplugged his Telecaster and made his way to Katie. "Let's get out of here. Now."

As they hurried off stage, they heard the comic. "Someone forgot their meds this morning. Sheesh. I feel sorry for his girlfriend. Hey, Rick? Maybe next time we should book the Happy Seven?" The crowd laughed.

Backstage, no one messed with the band. The bouncers and security were eerily quiet. "I think they're going to let us go and whack us on the way home," Nick said, trying to defuse the tension. It didn't work.

They rode back to their hotel. The phones didn't ring. No one came after them.

"You're still alive," Nick said to Becka when he go to their room. "They didn't take you out."

"Not yet," she said. "I think the band is too public a figure for them to try anything."

"So you think it worked?"

"Perfectly."

"Suckers."

Becka showed him her phone. "The net is going nuts. Diz is back. Diz still has the biggest balls of any band. That was awesome."

"We won," Becka said.

Nick shook his head. "Not yet. We're just getting started."

★★★★★

Later that night, as he slept, drunk on wine and his successful subversion, Nick dreamt. Rick Ross sat against a wall a lone, broken man. He wept. Nick almost felt bad for him. He heard the man whimper. "I just wanted to do good." Then the shotgun blast. Rick Ross's head turned into a gorey stew of red and black and blues. There were many grain-sized pieces stuck to the wall, and in Nick's mind's eye, he zoomed in on one and could tell it was a seed.

He smiled in his sleep.

"One of those was ours."

He laughed then.

"One of them was ours." ■

THE FIFTH CHAMBER

[Jake Marley]

We were told that only the very best people had a fifth chamber—an extra little pocket nestled in the right side of the heart that gives them the capacity for love and charity, kindness and humility—and that those of us without a fifth chamber weren't *exactly* monsters, nobody was calling us that, but we weren't exactly *complete*, either.

That's what Alexis, my sixteen-year-old daughter, said as her friends were ostracized at school and culled from the popular clique. Alexis demanded my wife and I set her an appointment so she could say for certain that yes, *of course* she had a fifth chamber…and she wouldn't have to be the next outcast.

There were a few tearful nights and one outrageous screaming match between Alexis and my wife Tanya where somehow the fight became a hurricane and I was swept into it and called a coward because I refused to weigh in with an opinion.

"What do you want me to say to her?" I asked my wife.

Tanya pursed her lips and gave me some serious side-eye as she gathered up her beaded, braided hair and tied it back, readying herself for the next battle in the screaming war. "There are girls at her school getting *surgeries.*"

"But it isn't real! Everyone knows there are only four chambers in a heart."

Tanya clenched her fists and shook them and said, "You can't look up from a book for a minute to open your eyes? Forget Alexis, I'll take care of her. You go watch the fucking news."

★★★★★

Coroners had been the first to notice. Dead men and women rolled into the morgues and one out of every ten or eleven people had a shared mutation. One article *dared* call the fifth chamber a deformity, and the comments section was filled with vile responses. I flicked through them watching the outrage build up steam and about halfway down the thread of hatred someone pointed out that the author of the article, Iman Malik, didn't sound like he or she was born in America, and I had to click away to the next article because it made me feel enraged and helpless. Not because I agreed with the commenters, but because it all sounded like so much horseshit to me.

Autopsies showed the fifth chamber to be a folded compartment in the right ventricle. One or two sites had long lists of medical terminology explaining it, but the words bled into nonsense as I tried to read them. Most others opted for metaphysics, discussing the *symmetry and balance* that the fifth chamber provided. It was hard to believe, but there were detailed photos of the hearts of the dead, with diagrams clearly labeled *unaltered anomalous behavior.*

Once the news spread and speculation rose about the chamber, then certain questionable heart surgeons came out

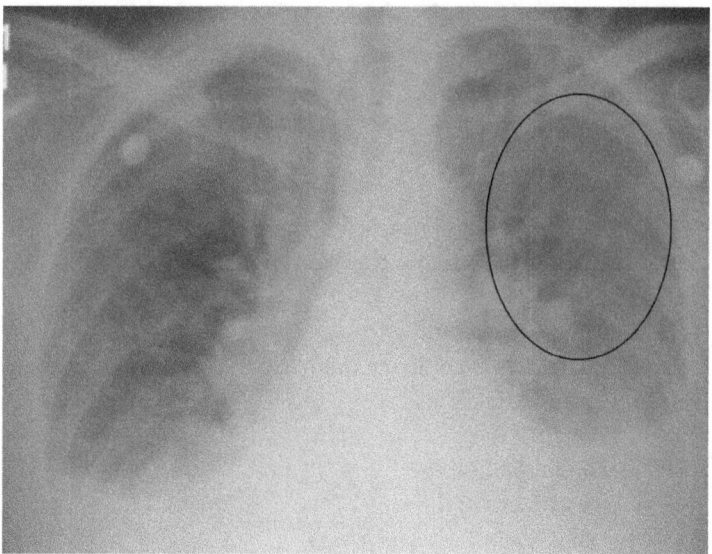

and claimed that they could give *anyone* a fifth chamber. Soon, they began advertising that it was *scientifically proven to increase a person's capacity to love*, although I couldn't find any research to back up the claims.

In fact, the *actual* scientific community denied it, but their rational statements were buried under page after page of radical websites. Misinformation blossomed to factoid-soundbites that seemed too thin and transparent to be believed. The religious right claimed fifth chambers for themselves, declaring them a divine miracle. *God-pockets*, they called them. They sent advocates to national events, held conferences, and filled social media with their proclamations.

Interest faded, written off as a quirky glitch in normality, until the president stepped up and publicly declared, "*Only the best of us have fifth chambers in our hearts. We've scanned the hearts of criminals and terrorists and they don't have them. Not one. The fifth chambers belong to honest, hard-working people. It's what makes America great. Don't let anyone tell you any different.*" There was no evidence of these scans, and no institutions, military or penitential, came forward to validate the president's claims. Soon after, though, surgical clinics began popping up in every major suburban area across the country. Little franchise shops, only instead of Subway sandwiches or T-Mobile stores, these were for cosmetic heart surgery.

"No fuckin' way," I said to my office. It was filled with books and a computer I'd disconnected from the internet in order to finish a book of my own and I had absolutely no idea that the world had gone insane when I wasn't looking. How had it happened so fast? How could I have missed it so completely?

The next article I read—this one written only a few days earlier—planted a seed of disquiet and unease that I couldn't shake. It was the first one that mentioned the *angelstones.*

I'd never been much of a journalist, but in college I interviewed local artists and local bands for a friend's burgeoning blog, so I searched online and made a couple of calls and ended up having lunch with Dr. Ryan Kincaid at a Five Guys burger stand by his office in Costa Mesa.

It was a gray day in California, threatening rain, and the palms were tilted in the strong breeze. Cars cut each other off in the parking lot, honking and throwing middle fingers out windows, and honking again before peeling out of the lot and onto the road. Just sitting by the window, watching the street from the corner of my eye, I saw three near-accidents.

"We're popping up like Starbucks," Kincaid said.

He was a round-faced man with smooth, apple-red cheeks and small, glistening eyes. His hair was very black, and the skin at his temples and on the tip of one ear was stained dark blue from the dye he used. His hands were small and creased and crushed complimentary peanut shells by putting three in his palm and rolling them together, then picking out the broken peanuts bit by bit.

"It's still a major surgery," Kincaid said, tapping his breastbone with a gaudy-gold class ring. "Gotta get through the ribs, but once you're in it's just a few snips and a pinch and they're as good as gold. Five-Cs are my bread-and-butter, but I'll do a few stents now and again, just to keep myself fresh in case the fad ends."

"And the stones?" I asked. "Do you add those in?"

Kincaid's body shook and his laugh was a little wheezy. He grabbed the straw of his milkshake and yanked it up and plunged it down obscenely before pursing his lips and taking a long, thick sip. "The stones aren't from us. They're like gallstones or kidney stones. They occur naturally." He leaned in close, licking drips of vanilla from his fingertips. "But I'll tell you something, off the record. I've got a guy in China who usually makes hippins, but he's going into the business of artificial stones. You can get them personalized with Bible verses, or the names of your kids. They're pricey, surgical-grade, but so much more tasteful than a tattoo, am I right?"

I'd lied to him on the phone. He thought I was writing something for the *OC Register*. I took notes, but half of my brain was thinking about my daughter. How could Alexis not see right through this? How could she think it was a good idea?

"Top heart surgeons shouldn't have any trouble getting work in this country, but those of us who don't have the right connections are seeing a benefit in providing this service. If you've been online, you know how Americans feel about the Five-C. All over the news, they say that only the best of us have 'em, but why should that be? It's not just cosmetic, like some detractors would have you think. Things line up when you've got one, naturally *or* with medical assistance, and let me tell you, it's transcendent. Truly life changing."

"So you have one?" I asked.

Kincaid nodded emphatically and tapped his chest with that class ring again. "Oh, yeah. Only the best people do."

I met my friend Greg later that day. The breeze had carried the gray clouds away, and the sun made the world sparkle and shine like a waxed car. We were at a cafe near his house, surrounded by the smells of brewed coffee and some acoustic Elvis Costello in the background. Greg was horrified when I admitted that I'd only just heard of the fifth chambers because Alexis was being bullied at school.

"Bullied because she doesn't have one?" Greg asked.

"Because she doesn't *know*."

Greg looked down at his hands, swirling the coffee in his cup. "Makes sense. We're subhuman to them."

Greg always looked like he'd stepped off the pages of GQ—well-dressed and untainted by the world around him, but now he was on edge. He set his coffee down and looked right at me, lowering his voice a little so we wouldn't be overheard by the people at the next table.

"We're the *tragic majority*. Nick's mother recently discovered she has a fifth chamber. You have to know, she's always been supportive of us in the past, but now it's like she's a completely different person. Like she no longer has to pretend to care. She actually told Nick that while she still loves him, she feels in her heart that she can't love his *lifestyle* anymore. Like he chose to be born gay, or that she hasn't known since he was six. She was never purposefully mean like that before she became one of *them*. I just don't get it. She talks of love and compassion, but she breaks Nick's heart every time we visit. They used to have such a close relationship."

"What about you guys?" I rapped on my chest the way Kincaid had earlier. "Are either of you rockin' a Five-C?"

Greg shook his head. "Nope. And before you ask me something obliviously insensitive or asshole-y, it's not because being gay makes us ineligible for one, either. Nick's ex has a fifth chamber, and that guy's a walking stereotype. Some of our friends are getting cut open to put one in, because…well, things are getting a little crazy, and everyone wants to fit in, right?"

"You thinking about having it done?"

Greg laughed in a way that always made me want to laugh, too. Like the whole terrifying world was just too damned funny. "Oh, no. No thanks. I'm plenty capable of loving and being loved without having a surgically-deformed heart."

I picked Alexis up at school, watching the way her "friends" circled her like vultures, cawed like ravens. Alexis walked with her head down until the girls nudged each other and broke away, falling on Jemma, one of Alexis's best friends since second grade. Jemma ran away, tears rolling down her face, and I was shocked to see these high school girls chase after her, shouting and chanting.

In the car, hiding from the girls, Alexis wouldn't look at me.

"They seem extra bitchy today," I said.

Alexis clenched her jaw. "It's because they're better than us, Dad."

"You don't know that."

"*They* do. They've been bringing their scans into school, to show everyone. They have the fifth chamber. Amber even has a *stone*."

"How many of them have surgery scars?"

The violence radiated off my daughter like heat from a bonfire. "You're being ignorant. Chambers by *choice* are our right. We can get them if we want, and we're still accepted."

"I find that hard to believe. Every subculture has a pecking order."

"Faith doesn't have a pecking order, Dad."

"Faith?"

"Not that you'd know anything about it. You don't believe in anything but your books."

My fists clenched around the steering wheel. My face pulsed with my heartbeat.

"What do you believe in, kiddo?"

I was baiting her. I was creating what Tanya would've called a *situation*.

"I believe in the power of love, and decency, and compassion, and that the only true way to get those things is through your heart. There is power and light and it resides in the fifth chamber of every true and perfect heart."

She sounded brainwashed. My little robot daughter.

"What about believers without a fifth chamber?"

"They're tragic, and need to be pitied." Alexis shrugged. "But they can get that fixed now. Heather said it was easy. Madison was back in school after only three weeks. Amber says they're among the chosen now."

"Amber knows everything, yeah?"

"She's one of the Naturals, Dad. *With a stone!* She's better than everyone, and so yeah, she knows. I could be just like her and not even know it because you and Mom are being *difficult*."

"What about Jemma?"

Alexis shrugged her shoulders and made an exasperated sigh. "She's so stupid. She actually told Amber that she *didn't* have a fifth chamber. She wasn't even embarrassed."

"And you just stood there and let them pick on her?"

"You're clueless. I can't even talk to you." Amber crossed her arms and stared out the window as I drove home. As we pulled in the driveway, she finally turned to face me and I was scared by what I saw in her eyes. "She *asked for it*, Dad. If she didn't want to get bullied she never should have told them. She deserved it. I would have yelled at her too, if I knew for sure that I've got one. I can't believe you won't let me get scanned."

I clenched my teeth. Made a decision. Something about hearing my daughter's words contradicting the tears rolling down Jemma's face. It made me sick.

"You'd better get used to waiting, kiddo. I will never pay for one."

★★★★★

She didn't fight. Didn't argue. I congratulated myself for being a good dad.

74

Even Tanya was impressed. We ate dinner as a family for the first time in months. There was a calm between us. Peace.

Alexis cut herself that night. She used the filet knife in the kitchen. The wound was deep and bloody and we barely got her to the ER in time for them to save her.

"*I need to know*," she'd screamed. Our baby, covered in blood. "*I need to know!*"

Tanya and I held hands in the waiting room, and we cried, and we were sick about the future.

★★★★★

Hector was an old friend from high school. He was a forensic scientist, and had access to all kinds of weird shit. When I asked him about angelstones, he'd told me to stop by his lab in Fullerton. He held a stone in a gloved hand and said, "Kind of looks like a Jordon almond, doesn't it?"

"What's a Jordon almond?"

"The little candied almonds they give out as wedding favors. They're crunchy, pastel colors. They bring good luck. You know."

"Sure," I said, but if I'd ever seen a Jordon almond, I hadn't known that's what it was called. "Can I hold it?"

"Gloves," Hector said.

"Such a small thing," I said. It was heavy. *Dense*. The weight of it was substantial.

"And *bizarre*," Hector said. "This one was taken from a corpse about a month ago. There's a good chance the guy was killed for it, and the perp—they think it's his son or his son-in-law—carved the stone out and tried to swallow it, but he kept throwing it up. Over and over again. Like seven or eight times."

He saw the look on my face and laughed.

"Don't worry, dude—I've cleaned it."

It was smooth, white, ovoid. "How do they form?"

"Nobody knows."

"What're they made of?"

Hector grinned. "Again, nobody knows. They're biological, but not registering. They just appear. Like the fifth chamber. One day you're clear, then next it's there. It's all a big mystery, but they obviously have something to do with each other. I mean, that's the only explanation."

"You're serious?"

He shrugged. "Pretty exciting times. Scary as hell, but exciting!"

★★★★★

While repairing her, they'd found an angelstone in our daughter's heart, about the size of a Skittle. I had tried to get the surgeon to remove it, but he told me it was her legacy. Her *right and privilege*. "She's better than the rest of us," the ER doctor said. "We'll see what she has to say on the subject."

She had her scans, and she had her scar. When she was well enough to return to school, the girls weren't circling her. They were *following*.

Tanya blamed me, I think. But at night we held hands as we listened to our daughter talk on the phone in the other room. Every word Alexis said sounded hateful and condescending.

"A Jordon almond," my wife said. I'd told her Hector's comparison a few weeks ago, and it must've resonated with people because that's how everybody thought of them now. Like it was candy, and made the owner somehow sweeter. In the last few months everyone with a fifth chamber now had a stone, even the ones who'd had them created surgically. Smooth, white, ovoid. "How could something so small mean anything?"

I squeezed her hand. My fears were deeper. Things were way past serious.

I told Tanya my theory. It had been building in my mind, but I kept pushing it away. I kept remembering how *heavy* the stone had been.

I told her the angelstones didn't look like almonds to me. They looked like eggs.

Tanya sobbed, but I couldn't stop talking. I had to say it aloud, to lay out the future of our world that I couldn't help but see. I had to let it out before my own heart would burst with it.

"If they're eggs," I said, "what's going to hatch out of them?"

On the other side of the wall, our daughter laughed—high and shrill, hateful and wild. ■

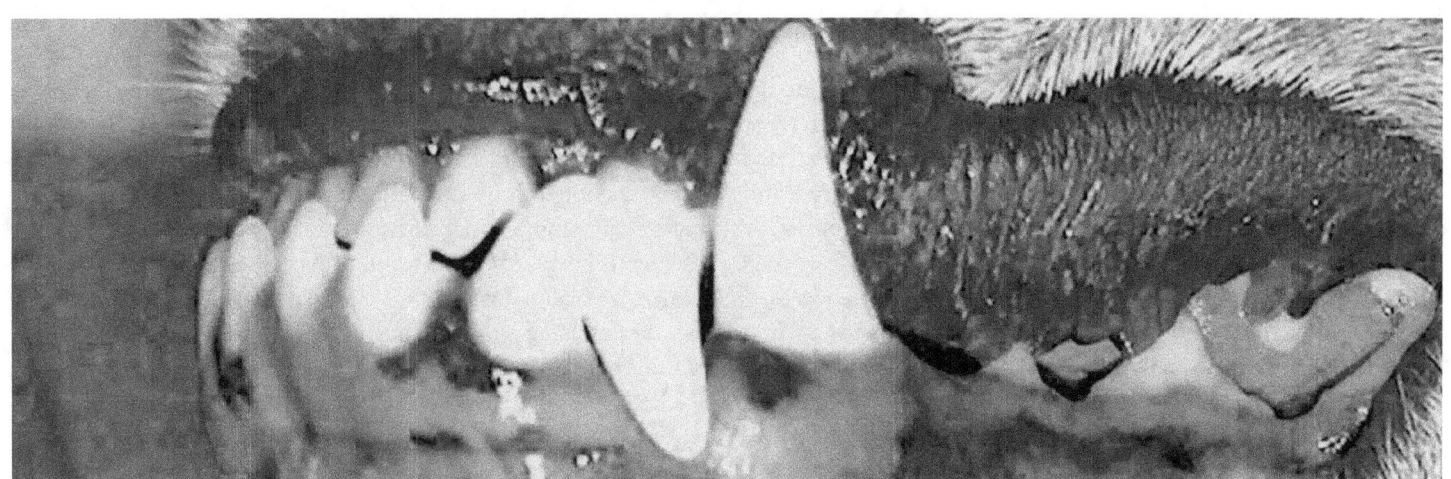

CANINE

[Jason A. Zwiker]

You see long jagged teeth, a loop of slobber, and rancid gums when he snarls. You point. There! But he's still and silent when your mama turns.

"Don't say that," she says. "Don't make up lies. That's mean."

You look again. One nostril is stuffed with a plastic tube, his eyes are closed, and the monitor by his hospital bed sketches out a slow, steady map of peaks and valleys. He rolled his truck three nights ago, that's about all anybody's told you.

"He was drinking," you say later, when you and your mama are in the elevator, descending. "Drunk."

You say it out loud. You're saying what you can see with your own eyes, hear with your own ears, piece together with your own brain. You say it like a statement but you're really asking a question. You're asking this question because you're just a kid and you want to understand.

"That's rude," your mama says. "That's not nice to say. You shouldn't say that when… when there's so much going on." She looks down, shakes her head. "Or ever. You shouldn't say that, ever."

There's a ding, the door slides open, and you're back on the ground floor.

Deep inside, you make a mental note: don't say out loud what you can see with your own eyes, hear with your own ears, piece together with your own brain. Don't say it. It's rude.

Why didn't he just die?

No more doors slamming, no more cowering as he drinks his way through a suitcase of Schlitz and announces to you and your mama that if anyone wants a war, he'll win.

And that's just how it was back when he still looked like a man. Before his snout grew long and his nose went black and wet. Before rough tufts of hair began to sprout between his knuckles. Before the rank smell began to linger along his path. Marking his territory.

"We should pray," your mama says, as she puts her Chrysler in gear and takes a right out of the parking lot. Slush, brown with grease and salt, lines the road on both sides.

You nod.

Silently, as the car slips through the winter wind, you and your mother both pray. Neither of you asks the other exactly what you're praying for. ■

THE MAN IN THE HIGH CHAIR

[Kurt Fawver, art by Nick Gucker]

For many years, there lived a man in a highchair atop the roof of our city hall. We had no idea where he came from, why he took up residence on our city hall of all places, or why he spent his days and nights crammed into a piece of furniture designed for infants. We could glean no answers from him, either, because, when he first appeared, he did little more than make funny faces at those of us on the ground—the kind you might make to a baby or the kind a baby might make to you. Day and night, the man sat above our mayor's office and pruned his brow and puckered his lips and blew out his cheeks and stuck out his tongue, and we strolled by beneath him, glancing up to see what crazy facial expression we might receive when we did. Perhaps too much like babies ourselves, we chortled and pointed and thought nothing of the man except that he was a momentary amusement, an entertaining distraction signifying nothing. Even our elected leaders, above whose offices the man had situated himself, made only the mildest of protestations against his residence, perhaps in a weak effort to curry favor with an electorate that seemed to appreciate the spectacle of the man in highchair far more than the safety of rational governance.

In those early days, if anyone did try to engage the man in the highchair in conversation, he simply responded with a string of incoherent and nonsensical syllables. "How's the weather up there today?" a passerby would shout—a favorite question of the commonfolk who thought they were being clever—and the man in the highchair would grimace and scream "Lawkerrup!" or "Maga maga!" or an equally meaningless jumble of sounds. We all thought it great sport to guess at the man's intent, even if we believed his words to be gibberish. The activity became so popular, in fact, that a drinking game sprouted up around the man's babble. On any given weekend night, it was common to see dozens of people standing beneath the man in the highchair, clutching paper bag-wrapped liquor bottles in their hands as they yelled out random questions and chuckled at their witty interpretations of the man's nonsense.

How the man received sustenance during his occupation of our city hall was a matter of some speculation. No one admitted to giving him food or water or, when the winter months blew in, heavy clothing and shelter, yet he never wanted for any of these resources. Indeed, as the years passed, he grew doughy and round from the sheer amount of creature comforts he somehow acquired. This corpulence led some of us to speculate that perhaps he'd hoarded food and goods in a secret locale and, even more, that he might have been climbing down from his chair during the wee hours of the night and stealing from our stores and our homes ever since he arrived.

Despite this potential criminal behavior, we didn't initially conceive of the man in the highchair as any sort of true threat. At worst, we thought of him as something akin to an embarrassing statue we had commissioned for the town but couldn't remove once it had been installed. This notion took on its greatest resonance when, one morning several summers after the man had arrived, a small glass tower unexpectedly appeared on the roof of city hall where he usually sat. Inside it perched the man, safe and comfortable on his highchair, wearing a goofy grin somehow less convivial than the ones he'd shown us in the past. Some of us whispered that the expression was almost menacing, but in a way we couldn't exactly explain.

Who built the man's glass tower and how they'd erected it so quickly and so covertly, without anyone noticing its construction, remained a daunting mystery. Surely, we rationalized, the man hadn't fashioned it by himself. Such an endeavor was beyond a single individual, no matter how skilled with hammer and rivet that person might be. But none of us stepped forward to claim our work or offer insight into the issue. It was almost as if the man had enlisted shadow contractors from an intangible realm to build his sparkling home.

Once the man in the highchair moved into his glass house, he dragged himself and his chair outside less and less. When he did emerge, it was only once or twice per day, for twenty or thirty minute spans. During these public appearances, the man no longer waited for us to ask questions, but squatted above us and, without provocation, shouted his nonsense words to the world in an unbroken torrent, the tone and cadence of which began to take on a dark edge—sometimes mocking, sometimes confrontational, and sometimes shockingly violent. Though we still had no inkling of the man's true intention or message, the venom of his insensible speech seeped deep beneath our skins, inflaming the marrow of our bones. Most of us shuddered at its implications and tried to purge it from our systems; others, however, embraced it, letting it ride through their veins and curdle in the chambers of their hearts.

Those who opened themselves to the man's empty but furious rhetoric soon began to act as though they'd been possessed by a spirit of blind vengeance. They walked about town hissing epithets at anyone who didn't look like them or talk like them or mirror the righteous flames in their eyes. They insisted on guarding public restrooms with firearms so that no one but themselves could use the facilities. In stores, they elbowed smaller and physically weaker people out of checkout lines and away from prime merchandise. Heated arguments over the man in the highchair's value to our community—or lack thereof—escalated into fistfights with regularity. And all about town, lawns suddenly sprouted metal poles, atop of which flew bright red flags emblazoned with golden highchairs. Faster than we would have liked to admit, a rupture had formed beneath us, and from its depths oozed a pernicious culture of unearned rage.

If the underlying pulse of anger that beat its way through the pavement of our town had been the sole symptom of the man in the highchair's newfound—and seemingly inexplicable—influence, we could have endured the discomfort and soldiered on as a unified people. But, little did we know it, anger and boorishness were to be only the first toxins to leach into our lives.

★★★★★

Not long after the rippling red flags began to occlude our stars, the man's glass tower underwent expansions—major expansions. First, it gained a more substantial foundation, which, when completed, filled the entirety of our town hall's roof surface. Then, it sprouted two wings that draped over the sides the hall and hung halfway to the ground like enormous, cubist icicles. Finally, it rose higher—roughly three times its original height, making it by far the tallest structure in our town.

Just as before, the parties responsible for the construction went unknown, with building taking place in the depths of night and proceeding with uncanny speed. We'd tuck in for a full evening's rest and wake to new, utterly completed extensions of the tower's reach. No screech of steel against steel ever split our sleep. No bright light that might indicate work ever emanated from within the tower's vicinity. No convoy of construction vehicles ever rumbled by our homes like a herd of stampeding bulls. The man's tower simply expanded, as though feeding off the fury of his adherents.

A few enterprising and inquisitive souls among us became so unnerved by this invisible workforce that they set up streaming video cameras in trees and bushes and streetlights adjacent to city hall in an effort to try to capture the builders in action. The results of their sleuthing, however, did little to dispel the mystery or pacify any of our anxieties. Most nights the cameras caught nothing; the tower stood rigid and imposing, but without any hint of growth. Other nights, at random points in time, an unusually undersized hand on an otherwise adult arm reached out from the darkness at the right edge of the video feed and grasped toward the cameras' lenses. An abrupt cut to what appeared to be a pile of writhing, half-charred human bodies followed the grabbing motion. The stream then dropped and couldn't be reestablished. Every morning that followed one of these particular nights, we woke to discover that the tower had added new dimensions and new features. After three weeks of witnessing the same pattern of mind-numbing stasis and nocturnal horror show without any explanation to show for their efforts, the amateur detectives packed up their gear and backed away, defeated by the illogic of the entire experience. We were more concerned about the tower's rapid ascent than ever before, but, armed with the knowledge that it held to no laws or reason that we understood, we had no idea what actions to take or how to proceed in order to prevent it from clawing higher.

As the glass palace continued to encroach further into our world, the man in the highchair's supporters became bolder and more brazen. Every day, by the hundreds, they organized beneath the tower, setting up lawn chairs and picnic blankets and outdoor grills as if at a music festival or a tailgating event. They painted the man's nonsense words on huge posterboard signs and, snarling like rabid dogs and feral cats, held them aloft like oblations to a god. From an invisible vendor, they purchased miniature red flags adorned by highchairs, and these they waved furiously or pinned to their clothes. If an unfortunate wandered into the gathering without a flag, that person was forcibly removed from the city hall grounds, often with much shoving and literal arm twisting, if not a small amount of bloodletting.

When the man in the highchair finally made his appearances above the massed, flag-bearing throngs, they ceased all motion and listened to his inarticulate ravings with rapt attention. If at any point he paused during his "addresses," they took up his mantle, imitating to the last guttural inflection whatever verbal sludge he had just vomited upon them. In this way, the gatherings might have best been described as call and response religious services or Greek stage tragedies in which the chorus had nothing of consequence to say for itself.

Beyond the tower, the man's supporters began to exhibit far more distressing behavior. They walked about town parroting the man's bitter nonsense words and dropping them into conversation whenever possible. The same words sometimes functioned as verbs, sometimes nouns, and sometimes adjectives or adverbs—it seemed that their use was predicated on arbitrary factors, if it was predicated on anything at all. We questioned the supporters about their speech and tried explain to them that it conveyed no ideas beyond unchained anger, but this tactic invariably resulted in assault. No sooner would we level a criticism than the supporters would dissolved into blind rage, flailing out with their fists in an effort to dislodge teeth and break noses, to fill our mouths with so much blood that we could no longer dissect their utterances.

We reported these incidents to our local police, but they hid behind a thin blue smirk. They assured us our cases would be investigated. They told us that our lives would protected at all cost. They even went as far as to haul a supporter or two off to their station for purported booking. But as soon as we turned our backs to them, they snickered and winked and murmured amongst themselves unmistakable fragments of the man in the highchair's vicious garble.

With little other civil recourse left to us, we petitioned our mayor and city council members to remove the man in the highchair and his tower from city hall or, at very least, impose strict penalties on his supporters' increasing violence. To these requests, however, we received nothing more than mannequin stares and blank letters of response. It was as though the pulp of our elected officials had been completely cored away, leaving behind human rinds incapable of simple action, let alone serious aid.

All the while, the crowds beneath the man in the highchair grew thicker, more raucous. They burned effigies of faceless women, of papier-mâché dolls painted black and brown. They brought firearms to their gatherings and discharged them into the clouds in a war with reason itself. And when the man lumbered from his tower and spoke to them, they cheered and cried and pumped their fists in triumph. He held them mesmerized with his anti-rhetoric, his void tongue. He spouted his usual vitriolic nonsense words and the supporters below nodded in approval, clapping and roaring at random intervals as though they understood the man's intent. This led us to wonder: Did the man beckon his followers to him with a whistle only certain ears are attuned to? Was he speaking a language we couldn't hear? Or were his words merely a mirror for a formless malice that always already stirred within his supporters' chests? It was impossible to determine the truth.

As the crowds grew, so, too, did the tower stretch its vast wings. They spread high over our small city, in all directions. They hung above our business district, our hospital, our schools and our county jail. City hall itself became totally encased in glass, its entrances and exits blocked by dozens of thick panes. This same excessive layering we witnessed everywhere across the tower—now more a castle or fortress, in truth. The structure seemed to be growing on its own, hiding itself away beneath an infinite series of surfaces, making of itself a matryoshka complex. And inside, at the core of his bellicose universe, roiled the man in the highchair.

Between gatherings, we glimpsed him lumbering along many random corridors, screaming and snarling at invisible enemies, his jowls a quivering mass of ochre jelly. He moved about his tower without apparent aim, content to be led by momentary whim and desire. His highchair, which, at this point, had been gilded and encrusted with gems by unknown parties, stood sentry at the entryway to his sanctum. Even though his newfound power over nearly half our populace seemed to invigorate him and send him wandering through his glass labyrinth more frequently, it was in the chair that he still slept and ate and defecated.

With the man in the highchair's influence casting an ever-darkening shadow over our lives, we found ourselves at a crossroads. We knew we couldn't allow the man and his fanatics free reign over our town, yet we possessed no readily tangible means of resistance. Our peacekeepers had become corrupt, our politics had been rendered impotent, and our law was dissolving further with every acrid bawl that dribbled from the man's puckered mouth. We were, ourselves, the last line of defense against the insanity of the highchair. Knowing this, some of our numbers chose to organize and march against the man's supporters when they gathered. Armed with homemade signs and rhyming chants, these bold protestors went to meet the worshippers of the highchair and attempt a vocal opposition to the wrath that had ensnared our home. They left excited, energized, ready to throw their bodies forward as the sword of justice. They held their heads high and laughed—nervously, at times—about the surprise they'd give the man's supporters. We truly believed this was a step in the right direction, a step that mattered. We truly believed we'd reached a turning point.

As it turned out, we would never see or hear from any of those protestors again. We waited for them to return, to give us an update on the opposition effort, but they never did. When we went looking for them, we turned up nothing. At city hall, the supporters milled about as usual; at police central booking,

the on-duty officers dismissed us, saying no arrests had been made; at individual protestors' homes, cars sat unmolested and doors and windows remained locked tight. An unsettling shroud of normalcy hung over the disappearances. We prayed that mass vanishings weren't part of the new usual, but the usual, we were quickly learning, signified little more than the particular insanities we were willing to accept on any given day.

★★★★★

Soon after the protestors went missing, we sought outside aid, calling the state police and the FBI, not to mention friends and family members who lived outside our city limits. However, our calls could not be placed, and the line dropped to hungry, waiting silence whenever we rang outside parties. If we pressed the issue and continued calling, our phones returned thousands of strings of meaningless text message, then overheated and died. Social media apps and pages through which we could have made pleas for help mysteriously loaded blank, bereft of the option to post updates or message contacts.

With digital avenues rendered impassible, we took to our cars, our bikes, our feet. We tried to leave the man and his insane supplicants behind. But, as we found out, we couldn't. At the edges of our city there now sliced a colossal white wall that loomed over our tallest buildings and our oldest trees. The wall cut through highway and sidewalk, forest and stream. Where it stood, soil and stone had been violently rent, as though it had burst from a fault line in the earth. Its milky smooth surface glistened as though wet, reminding us of false teeth and glass eyes. When we reached out to touch it in hopes of scaling its heights, our fingers swelled painfully and our chests tightened. Breath came in short, rapid bursts and our vision blurred. We couldn't fathom how a structure—even one as bizarre as the wall before us—could affect us in the same way as an allergen or a venom, yet that was precisely the case.

Lacking resources to safely mount the wall and concerned about our health, we fled back to our homes. We needed to plan more diligently, to organize more comprehensively. We needed strategy beyond knee-jerk fear. So we met late at night, in our garages, in our basements, and we carved out paths to resistance, if not escape. We planned days of unified strike, sit-ins at government buildings besides city hall, and marches through our streets. The steam of revolution began to waft from our windows. But as we planned and prepared, as we made ready to collapse the order of aggression that had taken over our city, people from our ranks began to disappear.

Just as the protestors had, our non-supporter friends, neighbors, and colleagues vanished without sight or sound of struggle, without a goodbye or a message of despondent surrender. Rumors of tan military-style trucks prowling our neighborhoods under moonlight circulated through our numbers. More than a few of us saw a trio of blue-suited men with identical red-mottled faces staring at the homes of the vanished from nearby sidewalks or lawns. We even witnessed computer and television screens flashing momentary, almost subliminal, images of wild, puffy eyes and mass graves. When we added these incidents to the disappearances and weighted the value of their import, the math of implication resulted in a frightening sum.

Even knowing that we might be snuffed into twirling wisps of memory at any given time, we tried to continue living as best we could. We watched television and browsed the internet, but all stations and all websites had been reduced to a single live-streamed video of the main entrance to the man's tower. We slumped off to work and ran necessary errands, but when we ventured beyond our front doors, we inevitably encountered the man's supporters who, by this time, used his incoherent speech as their primary lexicon and spat hulking wads of phlegm in our faces when we failed to understand their anti-language. Any further perceived slight we made against these people brought down upon us a flurry of fists and boot heels. Those of us who defended ourselves with reciprocal force ended up being dragged away by law enforcement and, in all cases, erased from the world. As a last resort, we tried to take refuge in the asylum of literature, but every book in the city—indeed, even those in our own collections—had been, impossibly, scrubbed clean of words. Only a grim narrative of periods and question marks remained between their covers.

While we dealt with the travails of daily life under the man in the highchair's dominion, his tower spread out across our sky like a vast crystalline mushroom cloud, blocking the firmament with a multifaceted glass ceiling. We could barely see the sun, the moon, or the stars without the lens of the man's tower distorting our view. We could barely see anything but the tower, hanging over us every hour of every day. And still our ranks were sucked into oblivion by cloned men in blue suits. And still the man in the highchair vented noxious sentiment into the atmosphere and our vital institutions. And still the man's supporters rallied to his tower and pledged allegiance to his maniacal bluster.

Now here we are, glass wholly encasing our world, the man in the highchair a step removed from godhood, and ourselves shades of the people we once believed. We know what we must do if we are to survive—the only course of action left to us. We must pick up the heaviest rocks we can carry, the most solid bricks we can find, and we must throw them, hard and fast and far and true. We must launch them from slings and catapults and homemade cannons. We must not be afraid of the sound of shattering glass or cracking bone. We must not worry about the grievous wounds we are sure to sustain. The man in the highchair and his adherents have chosen to destroy us, to remake our city as Pandaemonium. They cast the first stone, the second stone, every stone. Now let us cast our own. Let the man in the highchair be sliced to ribbons when his grand palace splinters above his head. Let his followers take cover and hide as we've had to hide or let them face the same mincing hail. Let us dance in the shower of glass and know we are free. This is our plan. This is our hope. We must succeed so that our city serves not as a forgotten tragedy or a cautionary tale, but as a legend of resistance for ages to come. ▪

Awesome word art by Thom Davidsohn